# The
# Vendetta
## of the
# Gods

African Mythology

*"Those who mediate when the gods are at loggerheads*
*are the demigods, and not eggheads."*

by

Philip Umukoro

RoseDog❧Books

PITTSBURGH, PENNSYLVANIA 15238

RoseDog Books
585 Alpha Drive, Suite 103
Pittsburgh, PA 15238
Visit our website at *www.rosedogbookstore.com*

ISBN: 978-1-63867-407-8
eISBN: 978-1-63867-508-2

# Preface

Theater in ancient Greece was an incontrovertible tool for social justice, cohesion mobilization, conscientization, and education. So, it is most likely you know about Zeus (the Greek god of thunder and justice) who ruled superior over other Olympian gods like Athena, Poseidon, Hades, and so on.

Similarly- (even although the majority of African countries did not develop one or more particular written tools to document their cultures and make them accessible enough to other continents as a result of some sort of language barrier, which was a huge problem before the European encroachment on African soil, hence more of these cultures were not known beyond the shores of Africa, and these "shortcomings" might have made it seemed that the African continent was demographically separated from the rest of the world), however, the oral repertoire of storytelling through the tradition of the griot was maintained and passed on to one generation and the other. In fact, this art (which stressed on the atavistic tendency of communocratic bond amongst the villagers) was as old as the primordial man. Therefore, we cannot overrule the fact that it was agriculture that gave birth to ritual, and then ritual to myth and folklore through sympathetic magic initiated by the early man when he went about hunting and farming.

Polemically, African philosophy (which was quite unlike its counterpart in another continent) was primarily based on traditional beliefs of the people, and it was habitually embellished in the hybridization of a wide range of cultural textuality of oral repertoires that would inform or teach the younger generations about the norms of their society. And this is evident across the African continent. More precisely, the Ballads, of the Zulu; the Legends, of the Ashanti; the captivating folklores of East and Central Africa; (etcetera, etcetera), are age-long practices that are meant to remind the people how far they have come culturally and socially.

Telling African stories does not confine to one particular theatrical dogma or convention alone. Otherwise, it defiles total regard for such a strict convention of the Aristotelian principle of "three unities." African oral tradition is an ensemble artwork in its entirety. However, the cause-effect technique is a unique element in Oral Repertory Theater.

It is probable that the Aristotelian convention of three unities and Hegelian logic of cause-effect technique truly gave way for Elinor Fuchs' "The Death of Characters," or Barthes' "The Death of the Author," or Foucault's "Death of Man;" or even so, Lyotard's "The Dissolution of the Metanarratives" (these writers who were also post-modern apologists in their own right), but one thing that stands in my perception is that I am not pressurized, furthermore than I intended, on what should be the basis for evaluating dramatic theatre in my dramaturgy. Shakespeare's Polonius' view concretizes my school of thought when he offered a famous testimony on "liberty to write in whichever way one seems to write."

 Hence, my dramaturgy is crafted in everyday language (simple but sublime) and aimed to teach and also make social commentary on everyday happenings. More succinctly, the African view of communicative conceptualization (before the pre-colonial era) was aimed at the achievement of cosmic totality—the meeting point of the people's rich cultural heritage, norms, and artistic ingenuity which could only be driven by a unified language. Because language, as they say, is a weapon and, also, a vehicle for social cohesion. It is an emblem that identifies one culture of people from the other.

Mythology or folklore can be arguably surreal or ethereal, but because of the pleasure they bring, writers will keep writing in order to keep the culture alive.

According to Yoruba folklore, Sango, and other gods (which include: Eshu, Ogun, Obatala, etc.) are deified because of the act of justice and vengeance they stand for among the Yoruba pantheon of gods. The Yoruba people believe that these gods have their different powers and functions (that are mainly exclusive to each of them), but at the end of the day, everything boils down to uphold justice for the oppressed. Thus, this art is an age-long tradition that is also peculiar to the African people before the pre-colonial and post-colonial eras. Moreover, the commercialization of the theatre in the thirties and forties did not do less to what the theatre is known for. But today, the theatre has been dwindled due to the lack of total commitment of some writers.

It is pertinent to know that this play *"THE VENDETTA OF THE GODS"* is chiefly inspired and crafted from Yoruba folklore.

Yoruba is one of the vast ethnic groups with a variety of cultural and historical records in western Africa, mostly in Nigeria. The people are unique, culturally groomed, and above all, they are the most educated among the other ethnic groups.

The Yoruba mythology is cut across other regions of the world, chiefly in many of the Afro-Caribbean countries like Cuba and Trinidad and Tobago, due to the transatlantic slave trade era. These two countries, and many others, worship Sango and other gods, respectively, which are originally from Africa. Therefore, one would be tempted to say that Africa is the home of mankind. Who knows? It could be true!

But mind you, mythology is a vast cultural entity that no one can lay claim that he has done justice to it; therefore, there is no need to explore any further. This is because there will always be a similar cultural identity of one region and the other and, of course, the people who feel they have not done justice to their folklores; or those who have not even written one piece of their folklore, would they not be interested to explore more and share their stories with the world?

I am not saying my story is the most pathetic because I have not told mine yet (not until now), and probably you have not heard or read my version (not until now, too) despite countless versions on the same theme around the world. So, it is not rocket science to be logical while critically evaluating any work of art.

Be that as it may, the intentionality of this play, "*THE VENDETTA OF THE GODS,*" is grossly based on the craftsmanship of myth or folklore to fit into current happenings in the society, so that what makes us Africans will not go into extinction both culturally and politically.

Furthermore, the play reflects vividly on socio-political and socio-cultural anomalies that are prevalent in the world and more particularly in Africa. Thus, the viability of theatre and drama as a veritable tool for social commentary with the intent and purpose to effect changes in society is inarguably never in doubt. Since social thought is concerned with the idea of humans as they relate to one another in a given environment, the playwright is therefore concerned with his social environment and how he would be of help to bring about substantial change (through his artworks for the betterment of all).

A playwright's ideology is hinged on the intentionality to right the wrongs of socio-political, cultural, and economic maladies in his immediate environment. This is because there is a symbiotic relationship between a playwright and his society, hence he is a part of current social thought he shares both in the problems and the blisses his society tends to present at any given time.

# Historically

In the creation year (when Tigers used to smoke), Eledumare—the Creator—gave Obatala (god of creation and laughter) the mandate to create every mortal—but not without displeasure put forward by other gods, chiefly by Sango (god of thunder and lightning), Ogun (god of iron and war), and Eshu (god of mischief and gatekeeper of the forked path). In the long run, something tragic happened which birthed a grave animosity the gods have for one another to date.

It is pertinent to know that Obatala was bewitched at the eve of creation by Egbere—a diminutive gnome—who transformed into a beautiful woman and then seduced him to get drunk—he became so drunk in love and on palm wine on the eve of creation. Can you imagine? As a drunk, he was, he began to carry out the task of creation entrusted to him by Eledumare. Consequently, the blinds, the albinos, and the hunchbacks were the aftermaths of his drunkenness. Pity, why not!

And what does this tell you? This simply means the task of creation Eledumare gave Obatala was an enviable one, so every other god was equally interested in championing the cause.

# Synopsis

THE VENDETTA OF THE GODS portrays an iconic struggle which tears the "Orishas"—"Gods"—apart; basically, the cosmic eruption between Sango (god of thunder and lightning) and Obatala (god of creation) after the eve of creation.

Obatala has become the king of Ile-Ife, and his kingdom is prosperous and peaceful. Meanwhile, Sango has also become the third king of Oyo after the previous king, Ajaka, had been ousted by the Oyo Mesi—council of chiefs—for his insubordination.

Quintessentially, Sango, who is always a power-drunk, becomes envious and vile when he hears about the prosperity of Ile-Ife under Obatala. So, he conspires with Eshu and Ogun to plunder Ile-Ife in broad daylight. Sango kills both high and low, imprisons Obatala, and then pronounces himself as the new king afterward.

To be frank, the play is a true reflection of Africa's socio-political system that is built on conspiracy. For instance, Sango, Eshu, and Ogun can be likened to bad political leaders who force their way into leadership and start oppressing the vulnerable for personal gain.

The play builds to a compromising point of concern, where Oyeyemi, whose pregnancy is long overdue, is unable to give birth because Obatala, who is the god that gives children, is still in prison at Sango's palace. Therefore, until

Obatala is released, Oyeyemi will remain in that predicament. And so do other pregnant women in the kingdom.

Ilesanmi (Oyeyemi's husband) says he will go and confront Sango and his allies and then free Obatala. But Langbodo cautions him that it is only a demi-god who can bell the cat and not mere mortal man. Then who will mediate between Obatala, who is the god of creation and laughter, and Sango, who is also the god of thunder and lightning? This is the question on everyone's lips.

This play hammers on the following themes: envy, oppression, vile, revenge, conspiracy, perseverance, and many more. As you read this unique and suspense-filled piece, you will see that folklore is so vast for any literary enthusiast to plunder without being slavish.

A fighting scene is also a critical point in a play that requires strict guidelines. It is always intense in its entirety. And every actor on stage must be mindful of this surrounding. Therefore, it pertinent to note that each fighting scene in this play is most likely to be choreographed for judicious use of stage management, space, time, and action. Above all, to avoid a minor mishap. Nevertheless, the show must go on! And also remember that in acting, there is no small role but only the small actor.

N.B. There are some Yoruba words, names, and towns that may pose difficulty in pronunciation, so I urge you (if you are unable to pronounce them properly) to disregard for smooth reading.

# About the Author

Philip Umukoro was born in Nigeria and obtained his Bachelor of Arts (Honours) in theatre and film studies at Nnamdi Azikiwe University, Awka. He is a critic and writer for a quite number of yet-to-be-published plays, poetry, and short stories.

Thank you!
March 2021

### For my late sister

*Ejiro, an angel who exited the stage of life*

*To sing hallelujah chorus amidst celestial beings*

*When her dew of life was still fresh*

*Like the rising of the morning sun.*

*Adieu, Ejiro!*

*If you can still telltale, do us proud.*

*Like how you left a vacuum in our mind's eye*

*And song of lachrymose on our lips, respectively*

*Greet your makers that had gone*

*On this same path where eyes of the living cannot pierce*

*Rest in peace, Imago Dei!*

# Dramatis Personae

*OBATALA (god of creation and king of Ile-Ife)*

*BASHURUN (Obatala's closest chief)*

*IYALOJA (woman leader)*

*SANGO (god of thunder and lightning; and the king of Oyo)*

*OYA (goddess of rain and Sango's wife)*

*ROYAL BARD (Sango's praise singer)*

*ESHU (god of mischief and Sango's friend)*

*OGUN (god of war and Sango's friend)*

*SUBJECTS (Sango's loyal subjects)*

*LANGBODO (herbalist and midwifery)*

*ILESANMI (unfortunate being)*

*OYEYEMI (Ilesanmi's wife whose pregnancy is long overdue)*

*OGUNDE (Sango's medicine man)*

*SUNYA (a fisherman)*

*BANJO (a fisherman)*

*AKALA (a blind medicine man)*

*TOWNSPEOPLE*

# Prologue

The actions in this prologue are intensely built on indistinct warring chattering and accompanied background rhythmic drumming.

Before the palace of Obatala, in Ile-Ife, a full-blown war has begun by Sango unannounced, who has left his Oyo for Ile-Ife and thereby invaded it with Ogun and Eshu. Parenthetically, Sango and his subjects have entered Ile-Ife

# The Vendetta of the Gods
# Movement One

Meanwhile, Obatala—who is the king of Ile-Ife—is seen on stage being flanked by two guards as he is attending to Iyaloja who has brought a couple of female dancers to be presented to the king for the forthcoming New Yam Festival.

OBATALA: *(addressing Iyaloja).* Are these the two female dancers you were telling me about yesterday?

IYALOJA: *(genuflects).* Oh, yes! As I said before, I am leaving no stone un-turned, Kabieyesi. As you can see, these girls, one light-skinned, the other her shade, are the fine ones selected for the choral procession of the sixteen Igbim drums, Kabieyesi.

OBATALA: Of course, by their looks I can see that their breasts are quite firm like an orange and their buttocks are well-rounded like a well-packaged pounded yam, respectively. I would love to say they are the souvenirs left for them when puberty came knocking at their doors. *(Laughing.)*

IYALOJA: You can say that again, Kabieyesi. Besides, you can see that they can no longer linger for the festive period to begin. *(Smiling broadly.)*

OBATALA: *(chuckles).* I am glad to hear that. May I see a preamble, at least?

IYALOJA: Aah, of course, Kabieyesi! These two are always ready to be wriggling their charming waists here and there like a pendulum of a grand-father clock!

OBATALA: (gladly). You do not mean it?

IYALOJA: I dare not lie to you, Your Majesty.

OBATALA: Whoa! Well, I must say I am impressed with your never-ending loyalty, Iyaloja. (Laughing.)

IYALOJA: It is a great honor to serve you, my king.

OBATALA: (sighs deeply). Hmm! It gladdens my heart!

IYALOJA: (Now calling and gesturing with a clap to assemble the girls.) Maidens!

[The maidens begin to showcase a few rhythmic dance steps, which gladden the hearts of Obatala and that of Iyaloja, as both begin to smile broadly.]

[Presently, a guard runs in to whisper into Obatala's ear. Obatala gets up from his throne, halts the dancing activity, and then begins to walk to and fro in a restless state.]

IYALOJA: (nervously). Is everything all right, Kabieyesi?

[Entering, Bashurun.]

BASHURUN: (walking in wearily while holding his cap in horror). Kabieyesi o! Kabieyesi o!

OBATALA: (turns quickly towards Bashurun). Bashurun?

BASHURUN: Kabieyesi o! (Bows.)

OBATALA: What is the news I hear that Sango of Oyo, my lone friend, who knows the craft of spitting fire like a wild dragon, is invading Ile-Ife?

BASHURUN: *(cuts in with his mouth widely opens).* Argh, Kabieyesi! It is no longer news. I saw Sango with my own two eyes killing the villagers—both high and low—like the bird flu. So Kabieyesi *(mumbling)*, I-I doubt if Sango still savors the taste of friendship how I saw him slaughtering the villagers at will. *(Demonstrating how Sango was killing the villagers.)* It was a grievous and inglorious sight to behold, Kabieyesi.

OBATALA: But you cannot be too sure, Bashurun?

BASHURUN: I am very sure about what I saw, Kabieyesi. *(Tearfully.)*

OBATALA: Horror! *(Frenzy).* Sango o! *(Now folding his arms in bewilderment.)* Awuu!

*[Presently, a messenger runs into the palace with machete wounds to inform Obatala to take caution.]*

MESSENGER: *(storming in amidst an awful countenance).* Fly, Kabieyesi! Fly! *(Now he crushes beneath Obatala's knees amidst tears.)* In the name of Orisha Oracle, fly, Kabieyesi!

OBATALA: I will not fly! I will do no such thing! Come what may, I will never abandon the dwellers of Ile Ife! It was never happened during the time of Olugbon of Igbo, neither in the time of Aresa of Iresa nor in the time of Oni-koyi of Ikoyi that a king abandoned his people in the time of trouble. *(Turns to Bashurun quickly.)* Bashurun?

BASHURUN: Kabieyesi o! *(Now dusting his cap intermittently.)*

OBATALA: Do you know that it has been a donkey's year that I have not seen my friend, Sango? Well, at least let me set my eyes on him again, and then offer him the best of wine! But my concern is, why would Sango, son of Oran-miyan, travel from Nupe—the home of his mother—and then arrive in Ile-Ife unannounced? Could it be a simple navigation error?

BASHURUN: I wonder, Kabieyesi.

*[Entering, Sango and others.]*

SANGO: *(from afar)*. You should, Bashurun! You should! Because a foretold war has never consumed the skull of a cripple!

OBATALA: *(acting surprised to see Sango and his followers)*. Aah! Aah! Sango, so it is you?

SANGO: It is me, Obatala. Who else conquers empires and enslaves the dwellers therein if not Sango? *(To his warriors.)* Seize them! *(Laughing cynically.)*

*[Bashurun, Iyaloja, and others escape taking the backstage. Meanwhile, Obatala is being captured alive, disrobed, disarmed, and then imprisoned. Hence, the throne, which overrules the people of Ile-Ife and over four hundred gods, has Sango now mounted and flacked by Ogun and Eshu. However, Eshu, in his characteristic nature, prefers sitting on a bare floor. Sango now bedecks his head with a kingly crown belonging to Obatala. The Subjects, each, find a suitable spot to sit on the floor which is carpeted with raffia mats.]*

*[Townspeople, entering wearily; they appear dumbfounded as they see Sango being bedecked with the royal paraphernalia.]*

*[Presently, the drumming fades off, giving the atmosphere tranquility for the characters to speak up.]*

SUBJECTS: *(in unison; they bow to Sango in homage)*. Kabieyesi o!

*[Sango becomes infuriated as he notices a cripple among the people in the palace.]*

SANGO: *(furiously).* Abomination! *(Calling.)* Guards?

*[Everyone becomes silent. Meanwhile, the Guard runs in.]*

GUARD: *(kneeling on one knee).* You called, my lord?

SANGO: Yes, I did. Get up! I am up here! *(He obeys.)* What is that thing crouching on the floor right there, at the trajectory of my hand. *(Pointing.)*

GUARD: *(looking where Sango is pointing at, and then thunders.)* Eewo!

SUBJECTS: *(upon noticing the cripple, they thunder in unison).* Argh, Kabieyesi, Eewo! It is forbidden!

SANGO: *(more furious, whirling as he thunders).* Executioner o!

EXECUTIONER: *(thunders and whirling before Sango).* Sango o!

SANGO: Take that thing out of my sight… and make sure you take care of him once and for all! *(Makes a killing gesture to the Executioner, then growls.)*

EXECUTIONER: Consider it done, my lord. *(Goes to the cripple, scoops him up, and dashes out.)*

CRIPPLE: *(screaming along).* Kabieyesi! Kabieyesi!

SANGO: *(straining his voice).* Take him away! *(Sharply turns to his Subjects.)* Is there one more person like that thing amongst you?

SUBJECTS: *(in unison).* No, Kabieyesi!

SANGO: Good! Obatala is a fool! I once told Eledumare—the Creator—that Obatala would bring doom to people like that thing, but he did not listen to me. *(Now gazes up as if he is talking to the Creator.)* Now, have you seen it? Have you, eh, Eledumare?

*[Executioner returning with his sword dripping with a bloodstain. He drips the blood inside Ogun's mouth. Ogun smiles broadly.]*

EXECUTIONER: *(turns to Sango sharply).* It is done, my lord. *(Now, he kneels on one knee.)* Is there anyone else?

SANGO: *(scanning the Arena again to be certain).* For now, I do not think so. *(To Executioner).* You may rise!

ROYAL BARD: *(cutting in to eulogize).* Kabieyesi o! *(From the rear end, thunders Sango's name.)* Sango, Oko Oya o!

*[Sango startles up: he moves here and there savoring his praise name while nodding in response.]*

ROYAL BARD: Whoever picks a fight with Sango demands his death unknowingly! Sango traveled to Ede and arrived at Ogbomosho. Aha! The secret of the anthill is never revealed, else man will no longer be overwhelmed by its designs. Sango is the cock that crows at the wee hours, that tells an ancestral spirit to depart the abode of the living. *(Thunders Sango's name repeatedly).* Sango o! *(Now, resigns solemnly.)* May you live long, Kabieyesi!

SANGO: *(quickly turns to the royal bard with a smile).* May that wagging tongue of yours outlive that of Olohu iyo of Owu. May you never stumble on a cactus on your worst day!

ROYAL BARD: Ase! It is so! *(Rubbing his palms against each other as a sign of affirmation.)* Argh, Kabieyesi, this is a great honor!

SANGO: I know. And I will not take it back... at least for now. Because your tongue is so sweet like a woman's lips. But still, I wonder why you have not taken a bride this far. *(Laughing deliriously.)*

ROYAL BARD: *(blurting out).* It is because of the fear of the unknown, Kabieyesi! The torture a man goes through in becoming a father scares me more than playing with a woman's nakedness, Kabieyesi! Eh! Besides, I am yet to see the Babalawo—medicine man—in the whole of Yoruba land who can assure me of the cure for rascality affecting the seeds dropping down from Eledua— the Creator—lately, Kabieyesi.

SANGO: *(turns to Townspeople to make jester of him).* Did you hear that? Did you? He has just earned himself another accolade. *(Giggles.)* But he is a fool! He almost succeeded in killing me with his rib-cracking foolishness. Awuu! Pity! Why not! *(Now he moves towards the audience with the horsetail waving high.)*

SUBJECTS: *(in unison, they thunder).* Kabieyesi o!

SANGO: *(raises his horsetail in response)* Eseun! Thank you! My people… *(boastfully)*, there are kings… and there are kids too. There are gods, across waters and lands, but I doubt if these gods can roar like me—Sango. It is not turning into a lion that is hard but getting the tail of it. Therefore, I am not just a king but a king with power! But for those of you who need to be reminded of who I am: I am Sango, son of Oranmiyan—the fire-breathing god. I, Sango, single-handedly invaded Ile-Ife and…

*[Eshu and Ogun cutting in with a feign cough and furrow their brows simultaneously.]*

SANGO: *(feigning a cough, too, then rephrases).* All right! I, Sango—with Eshu and Ogun fighting side by side with me—I invaded Ile-Ife in broad daylight, seized their king, Obatala, imprisoned him, and thereafter mounted on the enviable thrown of his forefathers. *(Laughing mischievously.)*

*[Eshu and Ogun smirk while nodding their head in admiration. Sango walks back to the throne, sits, and then turns to address Eshu and Ogun.]*

SANGO: *(shaking hands with Eshu, then thunders)*. Eshu o!

ESHU: *(thunders in response)*. Eeh o! *(Now wriggling his nose as he answers pungently.)*

SANGO: Eshu, the confuser of men at the forked path. *(Eshu is nodding in response.)* Eshu, who has a thousand stools but prefers to sit on a bare floor—I greet you.

ESHU: *(nodding in an affirmation)*. That is me, Sango.

SANGO: I know! *(Turning to his Subjects.)* A hunter once made the mistake of his life by asking Eshu if he had seen a bullet-wounded antelope wandering his path, and Eshu did not hesitate to tell him yes. And then went further to say, "The antelope went that way... *(Sango pointing left)*, no, that way... *(Sango pointing right)*, no, sorry, that way... *(Sango pointing upward)*." Thereafter, the hunter became so confused that he shot himself in the head. *(Now, to Eshu.)* Meanwhile, the antelope in question was in your weather-beaten bag. *(Laughing.)*

ESHU: I swear, I did not eat that antelope alone; in fact, I gave the big head to Ogun! *(Imaginary picking his teeth amidst laughter.)*

SANGO: *(turns to Ogun more properly)*. Aha! *(Thunders.)* Ogun o!

OGUN: *(thunders in response)*. Eeh o! *(Beating his chest afterward as he answers pungently.)*

SANGO: *(turning to his Subjects, now pointing the horsetail)*. A farmer had a cut with his machete and thereafter blamed his wife for over-sharpening the edge which made him bled. Awuu! Pity! *(Now then turns to Ogun sharply.)* Ogun, how daft was that very man... who forgot so soon that it was you who he had offended when he stole a sacred stone from your shrine at Owu? *(Ogun nods his head in affirmation.)* Ogun, who has a thousand pots of water in his oubliette, yet he prefers to bathe with blood. Now, I ask: what do you use water for, my good friend? *(Laughing jocundly.)*

OGUN: Huh! *(Jumps up sharply and then stares at Sango.)* Ah, water? Well, I am yet to know its uses. But in the time past, I had seen a man choked by it at Modakeke. But you know me too well, Sango, that when I am thirsty, blood I drink, and when I want to have a bath, blood at my disposal. *(Laughing sinisterly.)*

SANGO: Indeed. *(Laughing.)*

*[Entering, two of Sango's guards, who are marching a man and a woman into the palace amidst scuffles.]*

SANGO: *(getting up with rage, and then blurts out).* These guards!

GUARDS: *(they go down on their knees to pay homage).* Kabieyesi o!

SANGO: W-what! *(Walking to them and then gives both of them slaps.)* Fools! I can see that it has become a ritual for both of you to be bringing mad people to the palace whenever a kingdom is being conquered by me... *(turns to the Subjects),* Oyo was no lees. *(Now, he returns to the Guards.)* What is it this time?

FIRST GUARD: *(elucidating).* My lord, these fellows we brought before you are husband and wife...

SECOND GUARD: *(cuts in sharply).* But they were arrested just before they were about to commit an abominable thing, my lord.

SANGO: *(cuts in sharply and furiously).* And so? That is not my concern! You should have allowed them! Okay! *(Now, harshly towards guards.)* Up, up! Get out of my sight and make yourself useful. *(They obey.)* Good! *(Turns to the couple.)* I am Sango, a god, now second-in-command after Eledua—the creator. Who are you? *(staring at the man.)*

HUSBAND: I greet you, Kabieyesi. I am Adediran. I am an Ijesha man. And my father was the greatest palm wine tapper...

SANGO: *(cuts in immediately)*. Ah, ah, Adediran... son of Alapeni—the greatest palm wine tapper of his time.

HUSBAND: You are right, Kabieyesi.

SANGO: What a coincidence! I tell you, it was inevitably tragedy on that fateful day your father fell from a palm tree belonging to Irun male—the pantheon of gods—and met his death. Meanwhile, Olurobi, who is your mother, was heavily pregnant. But upon hearing the news of her fallen husband, she went into forced labor, struggled with her last breath, and then managed to push out two newborns from her vagina—a boy and a girl. Unfortunately, a few hours later, Olurobi decided to join her husband by taking her own life! *(Grunts deeply.)*

HUSBAND: *(affirming tearfully)*. Y-you are not far from the truth, Kabieyesi.

SANGO: Would you rather call me a liar?

HUSBAND: *(sharply)*. I dare not, Kabieyesi.

SANGO: My thought exactly. So, what was the quarrel all about, Adediran? Speak; Sango is all ears! *(Going back to his throne and sits.)*

HUSBAND: Thank you, Kabieyesi! *(Turns to his wife sharply.)* This woman wants to kill me, Kabieyesi! In fact, my wife wants to kill me before the time Eledua—the Creator—has given me on this earth. How can a woman keep nagging like a mad man who keeps threatening his fellows to stop calling him a "mad man?" Please do not get me wrong. I am not a fan of people who wash their dirty linen outside, but I cannot hide a dirty character either. Argh, Kabieyesi... my wife snorts every night like a pig! *(Feigning crying.)* And worse, she does not want me to marry a new bride after her. *(Sharply.)* But yesterday evening, Kabieyesi (*chuckles, now restrains*), I married a new bride with my money against all odds; by her look, you will know that she is an Ijesha woman—she is a fine choice, quite petite; her voice is melodious and thin like a thread, and when she moves her waist, Kabieyesi, it gives no care to the world as it sways here and there like the testicles between my thighs. But would you believe it if I told you that this woman here gave me the beating of my life from dusk till dawn, Kabieyesi?

SANGO: By her size, I would not think otherwise. But humor me!

*[Now, demonstrating the act of picking and slamming people on the floor.]*

HUSBAND: By nature, I am small in size, so she would carry me up to Eledua "freeeee-gbam" on the floor. And again, she would lift me above her head and "freeeee-gbam" on the floor. And again...

SANGO: (*cuts in quickly*). That would be enough, Adediku!

HUSBAND: (*tries to correct Sango for mispronouncing his name*). Adediran, Kabieyesi.

SANGO: Does it matter! (*Turns to the woman sharply.*) Woman... you are next!

WIFE: (*readjusting her wrapper*). I greet you, Kabieyesi. I am Aduke, and I am from this very land, Kabieyesi. (*Turns to her husband.*) But Kabieyesi, it was true that I carried Adediran, my husband, "freeeee-gbam" on the floor many times—no doubt.

SUBJECTS: (*laughing*). Ha, ha...

SANGO: (*thunders*). Silence! Proceed, woman!

WIFE: (*continuing*). Of course, it may sound funny, and then make you all laugh for the joy of it, but on the contrary, what I did was to teach my husband

11

a lesson for playing god with my heart. I am not done with him yet, Kabieyesi. I will so much deal with him to the extent that whenever he sees me, he would forget his surname when I ask him so. *(Turns to Adediran sharply)*. I warned you! Did I not? *(She holds Adediran by the ear tightly.)*

SUBJECTS: *(indistinctively dissatisfied with the woman's action)*. Argh... Kabieyesi!

WIFE: Oh yes! Kabieyesi, I warned this he-goat of a husband several times that I would not tolerate any idea of a co-wife, but he would not listen to me. Here is the deal—Adediran cannot satisfy me, let alone have another wife. Who does that, Kabieyesi? He should be ashamed of himself!

SANGO: Why should he, if I may ask?

WIFE: Because the walking stick beneath Adediran's thighs is too small to make a woman scream, Kabieyesi! *(Starts to feign tears.)*

SUBJECTS: *(indistinct chattering)*. Argh! Argh!

SANGO: *(thunders furiously)*. Silence! *(Exchanging chuckle with Eshu and Ogun at the interval.)*

[*Adediran now hides his face in shame. Meanwhile, Townspeoples are still silent amidst figuring out the circumstances that surround the earlier event.*]

OGUN: *(to the woman)*. Was that all?

WIFE: Not really.

OGUN: *(thunders)*. Then continue, woman!

SANGO: *(thunders)*. Do you think we have all day?

WIFE: *(quivering as she genuflects on one knee)*. My apologies, Kabieyesi!

SANGO: *(contemptuously)*. Woman, would you go ahead!

WIFE: All right, Kabieyesi! Our people say, "The hunter's dog that wants to get lost will not hear a sound of the whistle from the hunter." So, yesterday, Adediran, my husband, brought a new woman to our home against my stern warning. Oh, Kabieyesi, I was angry beyond what words could express, so I had to teach him a lesson he would not forget in a hurry! That was all, Kabieyesi.

SANGO: *(heaves a heavy sigh)*. This is a more difficult situation than I thought. But I have weighed both complaints fair and fair. So, these are my judgments… Guards!

*[Entering, Guards.]*

GUARDS: *(bowing)*. My lord!

SANGO: Up, up; I am up here. *(They obey, now to Adediran.)* I am angry with you Adediran, son of Alapeni. You see, you have disgraced manhood beyond what words could fix right now; I, therefore, think you should be taught a lesson, even more, than the one your wife has already taught you. This is because I cannot lord over Ile-Ife while an infidel rubs mud on manhood. Guards, take him away and give him ten strokes of the cane. And after that, throw him into the mines and make him work from dawn till dusk for three good moons and another three good moon after that and one after that!

HUSBAND: Argh, Kabieyesi, I will die!

SANGO: Of course, you will, but definatelly not today. Take him away!

*[The Guards begin to blindfold him*

13

HUSBAND: *(pleading amidst tears as he is being bundle out of the palace).* Argh, Kabieyesi! E jowo dariji mi! Please Kabieyesi, I beg of you!

SANGO: Take him away! Nonsense! *(They obey. To the woman.)* As for you, woman, you will stay here with me in the palace to serve your punishment. Do you understand me?

WIFE: I do, Kabieyesi. *(Genuflects on one knee.)*

SANGO: Good! *(Laughing broadly.)*

[*Eshu and Ogun join in in the laughter amidst exchanging few glances with Sango.*]

SUBJECTS: *(in unison).* Kabieyesi o!

SANGO: *(gets up, and then addresses his Subjects).* Eseun! Thank you! As you can see, the sun has gone home to rest. And it has also been a tough day for us all. So, I must retire now to have the chambers checked and as well lay down my head. Every one of you must also find a place to rest your heads. You have made me proud today *(urging his Subjects.)* So, go into the town and find any empty homes and occupy them—this is now your home! Good night!

SUBJECTS: *(in unison).* Kabieyesi o!

[*Sango's loyal subjects paying homage as they disperse alongside the Townspeople.*]

SANGO: That is the spirit*! (Turns to Eshu swiftly.)* Eshu o!

ESHU: *(springs up in response).* I have not left for my oubliette yet, Sango!

SANGO: Okare! That is the spirit! *(Now, turns to Ogun.)* Ogun o!

OGUN: *(springs up, too).* I have not also left for the Savannah yet, Sango.

SANGO: I know. *(Chuckling.)* Please, come with me, brothers... You too, woman! *(Obeys.)*

*[Sango takes a lead; follow suit—Eshu, Ogun, and the woman.]*

*CURTAIN*

# The Vendetta of the Gods
# Movement Two

*L*angbodo's house. A village under Ile-Ife province. The scene opens, ushers in Ile-sanmi and an able-bodied man struggling to carry Oyeyemi, whose pregnancy is long overdue, with a parakeet (a wooden stretcher), to Langbodo's house. Now, Ile-sanmi is calling: "Baba... Baba..." They drop Oyeyemi on the floor. The able-bodied man exits. Oyeyemi groaning pulsates at the interval.

ILESANMI: *(pacing up and down as he keeps calling)*. Baba...? Baba...?

LANGBODO: *(storms out with a talisman amidst a scream)*. Eeh o! I dare that man who wants my skull for a sacrificial scalp dance!

*[Becoming calm suddenly as he turns to the direction where Ilesanmi is standing.]*

LANGBODO: Ah, ah! Ilesanmi, it is you? *(Drops the talisman.)*

ILESANMI: *(bows)*. Yes, Baba, it is me. I need your help... Oyeyemi is dying, Baba. *(Pointing at Oyeyemi.)*

OYEYEMI: *(groaning)*. Hmm... Ikun mi o... Ikun mi o! My stomach... my stomach!

LANGBODO: *(exclaims loudly)*. Ah, ah, Oyeyemi... the seed of Obatala. Awuu!

No one pursues by death and dies in the house of Langbodo. *(To Ilesanmi.)* Wherever you see one tree standing there is another standing too. By the way, how long has she been in this misfortune?

ILESANMI: *(raises three fingers)*. Three days, Baba… three days.

LANGBODO: *(sighs deeply)*. Hmm! *(Now casting his Opele Oracle, and then begins to sing a mournful song)*. Adan 'k`ee o alaroye eye; i`ku o`kami l` eye adan`ke`. Ilesanmi, Ifa Oracle says I should greet you. Ifa Oracle says you have suffered a lot!

ILESANMI: *(exclaims loudly)*. Argh, Baba!

LANGBODO: Is it that bad?

ILESANMI: *(exclaims loudly)*. Argh, it is more than "bad," "worse," and even "worst" all put together what my eyes have seen, Baba!

LANGBODO: Oh! *(Casting the Ifa Oracle the second time.)* A bi lo'ode Ugbo o lo j'oba l'ode Iranje. Ah! Sango, jebureo, awo olugbebe o! *(Thunders.)* Sango, I pray you mercy!

ILESANMI: Baba? *(Now, mumbling)*. W-what has Sango got to do with my wife's predicament, eh?

LANGBODO: *(recasting the object of divination the third time)*. Hmm! If there is nothing so important on earth here, the eagle would not bother to look down for its prey. *(Observing the objects of divinity.)* Eseun! Thank you, Eledua!

ILESANMI: So, Baba, what did the Oracle say? Did it speak of evil? Speak to me, Baba!

LANGBODO: *(calmly)*. Ilesanmi?

ILESANMI: Yes, Baba.

LANGBODO: Listen to me, my son. Whenever you see a woman descending a sloping hill without both of her hands supporting her dangling breasts, then it is obvious that the trouble after her is a big one. You see, I do not want to deceive you—do you hear me, eh? Obatala, the god of creation, is in prison. What I am seeing here is nothing but a conspiracy. Conspiracy is at play again!

ILESANMI: *(nervous)* Conspiracy? What do you mean, Baba?

LANGBODO: I mean, Sango has imprisoned the god of creation. *(Looking at Ilesanmi pitifully.)* And I can see a spell…. I mean, Oyeyemi is under a spell. Therefore, until Obatala is released from the spell of Sango, Oyeyemi will never be free from her long-overdue pregnancy. Besides, in cases like this, she might die along with her seed once the moon becomes full.

ILESANMI: *(looking at the moon that is being drawn on the wall).* But, Baba, you just said, "No one comes to your house and dies."

LANGBODO: *(turns his back against him).* When did I say that? Okay. Now, I remember. But in her case, it is not a mortal man that wants her blood for the rite of passage, rather the gods. And as such, I am helpless like a man whose manhood has been chopped off.

OYEYEMI: *(continues groaning).* Baba… my stomach… I am dying. *(Turns to her husband.)* Ilesanmi… Ilesanmi, come closer… okay. Place your hand there… on my pubic. No… here. Now, swear by the water that just broke out of my womanliness that you will never commit suicide if the worst ever happens to me and this unborn baby. *(Shouts so loudly.)* Swear, Ilesanmi! Swear! *(Sobbing.)*

ILESANMI: *(pitifully).* Oyeyemi. *(Now sobbing as he turns to Langbodo.)* B-Baba… did you hear what she just said? I guess you did. She needs urgent help, please. *(Goes on his knees).* Oyeyemi must not die! Please save me from the world: I cannot face them and tell tales of what might happen to my household if you do not help! *(Sighs and then kneels before Langbodo.)* Baba, please, beg the Orisha on my behalf to save my wife and my unborn child. Please! *(Continuing sobbing, now, more uncontrollably.)*

LANGBODO: This is beyond me. So, I cannot save her. Rather, you are the one to save her and the seed in her womb—that is the only solution the oracle provided so far.

ILESANMI: *(startles up, then mumbling).* H-how Baba? Why me of such task?

LANGBODO: Listen, there are two ways to end this misfortune. First, Sango must be pacified, in order to avert the impending doom that is erecting its tent on our heads. Second, the Oracle says there will be a transmutation of souls at the abyss before the unborn can be born. Now I ask you: can you meet your death, Ilesanmi, for the rite of a new dawn? Transfiguration! Can you?

*[Ilesanmi suddenly becomes quiet and confused.]*

LANGBODO: Have you suddenly become dumb, eh Ilesanmi?

ILESANMI: I am not. I am simply confused like a man who sees a two-headed snake. But if it is Eledua's wish, then I have no choice but to do it. After all, what am I living for if not for the passage of the seeds in my testicles? *(Taking a couple of steps away from Langbodo.)* Baba, things might turn out this way to knock me off the reality of life, but I can still remember that I am the only surviving progeny of the first "Babalawo" in the whole of Ife kingdom. *(Mimicking the guttural voice of a masquerade as he dramatizes a dance.)* Baba, it is only the strong breed that knows where a masquerade lives. *(Thunders.)* Sango o!

LANGBODO: That is the spirit! *(Rolling out a drum.)* Now, you have to dance to the rhythmic Bata drum of Sango, Ilesanmi, because it is a tradition for anybody who is visiting Sango for the first time.

*[Ilesanmi hesitates a bit now; he turns and gives his wife a sad glance before he starts dancing as Langbodo hypnotizes him.]*

LANGBODO: That is the spirit! You are the true son of your father! *(Spits into a jar and gives Ilesanmi to drink.)* This is the first ritual that will aid you in the task ahead. When the gods are at loggerheads with themselves, those who aspire to pave way for their reconciliation are the demi-gods and not eggheads. Ilesanmi, you are about to embark on a perilous journey to settle the quarrel rapping the gods. *(The drumming abruptly stops.)*

ILESANMI: *(panting heavily)*. Quarrel? Who is quarreling who, Baba? And it seems you are beginning to scare me before my own very eyes, wise one.

LANGBODO: The gods are at loggerheads, but that is a story for another day. You can go home now. Oyeyemi will be safe here with me.

*[Ilesanmi goes and touches his wife as she resumes her groaning before he turns to go.]*

*CURTAIN*

# The Vendetta of the Gods
## Movement Three

Evening. *The scene opens in the market. All the people in the market are blind...* *Eshu enters with gourds of palm wine on his head. He stops at the market center, scans left and right with close observation. Presently, he opens the lid of the gourd which contains palm wine.*

ESHU: *(begins to gulp the palm wine).* This wine is becoming bitter... like sugarcane. No... like a bitter leaf. Wait a minute, must I also confuse my head, too? Whatever. Well, Sango and Obatala can be at loggerheads for all I care! It is their funerals, if they must know! Besides, I don't mind if Ogun calls me an ostrich for embracing the fence in this matter. But Ogun must know that I can no longer be fooled by Sango. The hunter thinks the monkey is not wise, yet he forgets that the monkey has its logic. I, Eshu... *(chest-thumping while looking at the market women)*, who amongst you do not know my praise name? *(No response).* I see. What insolent behavior! Okay! Well, we shall see!

*[Eshu throws a stone at one of them, which leads to the upheaval in the market causing pandemonium as the blind marketers ignorantly attack and accuse one another.]*

ESHU: *(laughing with satisfaction. Now, self-adulation).* I am Eshu, the trickster god and the gatekeeper of the forked path. I once confused a stranger from Modakeke who was heading to Ogbomosho. And, in my own very eyes, he committed suicide because he did not know which road at the forked path led to Ogbomosho. I, Eshu… *(sighs heavily)*, who once beat a child from Ede to Oshogbo, where the child's mother lived. When I got there, the mother asked what her child had done to warrant such beating. And I bluntly told her that I just felt like beating her child for fun, and right there, she collected the whip from me and then continued from where I stopped. *(Continues to laugh, now cynically.)* If I throw a stone today, it will drop on the head of a victim tomorrow. If the gods can never be wrong, then who am I never to salivate the suffering of these fools! *(Resuming laughing out loud.)* Who am I!?

*[Presently, Ogun enters from the opposite direction, bluntly spectating the pandemonium within the market women.]*

OGUN: *(soliloquizing).* This is serious! This must be the inglorious land of the Blind Eshu told me about, which, of course, is not far from his oubliette. But wonder shall never go to oblivion! How come Eshu could not leave that his wobble and shabby oubliette and come over here to settle these warring neighbors of his? *(Dropping the weapons on him, sighs, and then stands his hands akimbo).* But… but Eshu is kind-hearted and honest a man… *(pauses, then chuckles),* especially to things that are unconnected to this. *(Laughing as he points in the direction of the market woman as they disperse wearily.)*

*[Ogun picks up his weapons as he begins to cross over to where Eshu is drinking himself into a pulp.]*

OGUN: *(stopping after he has left Eshu behind with two laps).* That fellow… I mean, that short fellow, with a gourd raised to Eledua to have the content drained down his throat, has a shabby resemblance of my troublesome friend— Eshu. *(Now racking his brain.)*

ESHU: *(shatters the first gourd and then heaves a heavy sigh).* I am now drunk… so, any mischief I, Eshu, cause from this moment on, I am not accountable for it but the diminutive gnome of drunkenness that has taken over me. *(Staggering here and there.)* Wait a minute. That fellow… I mean, that tall fellow, with the weapons of mass destruction that were carried shoulder high, has a striking resemblance of my blood-thirsty friend Ogun. Where was I when he passed? *(Going back to a specific spot.)* Okay. I stood like this... while the gourd was as high as this position, and then, the fellow was coming... precisely from that point. *(Pointing amidst staggering.)*

OGUN: I think that fellow is not taking this path yet. Or perhaps, he has committed suicide with that which I saw him raised to Eledua. Well, I think it is not a bad idea if I go back to take a look at his funeral. *(Chuckling.)*

*[Dramatically, both of them begin to tiptoe backward till they bump and startle each other with a similar shout.]*

ESHU: *(turns back, thus he recognizes Ogun).* Eh! Ah, ah... Ogun, it is you? *(Moving closer to Ogun.)*

*[As soon as he recognizes the voice of Eshu, he quickly turns to respond.]*

OGUN: *(gladly).* Eshu, confuser of men, it is me, Ogun your friend.

*[They head-butt each other and then sit on the pathway drinking without minding the passersby who walk to and fro to their destinations. Eshu is pouring Ogun another round of wine, and within a second, he swallows it.]*

ESHU: Drink more... fill full, my friend. Because the spool that interwove the essence of life is the present. *(Passing the gourd to Ogun to satisfy his demand.)* I must say it is quite unfortunate for me since the vulture returned from the chthonic realm and met its death at Ogbomosho. *(Pauses a bit.)* By nature, I thought Sango would be different... at least, but I was wrong in my foolishness. I was wrong, Ogun! But... well, there is an adage people of this part usually say that I am fond of... kind of. They say: "The rabbit does not journey in daylight unless he has been visited by the snake in his burrow." So, tell me, Ogun, have you been well?

OGUN: *(belching as he drops the gourd).* Argh! I have been well, my friend, but not as my heart wishes. Eshu, do you know that if a child keeps pointing in a particular direction while crying, if the mother is not there, then there is something out of reach the child desires so much?

ESHU: *(affirms)*. My point exactly.

OGUN: Well, my mission is pregnant if you must listen to me.

ESHU: I am all ears, Ogun. *(He intentionally covers his ears)*.

OGUN: You never ceas to amuse me. Idiot! Anyway, Sango has yet again called for our help against some kingdoms whose warriors are hitherto beating drums of war to crumble his palace at Ife.

ESHU: *(fires up)*. And so? And you think I will honor yet again such bloody invitation of that traitor? I, Eshu, will not... one bit. Tell him that I had never benefited from any of his previous wars. War, war, war... no rewards!

OGUN: *(cuts in sharply)*. And you think I was different, eh, Eshu?

ESHU: Come on! At least the sales of your weapons in each previous war could make you a fortune. I must let you know... I am too old to salivate the business of war now.

OGUN: *(splitting a kola nut)*. Why, if I may ask? *(Now, he lobs a lobe into his mouth then starts to masticate.)* I know there are more which meet the eyes, my friend.

*[Eshu rises with anger smears all over his face.]*

OGUN: Be a man, Eshu! Tell me your grievances towards Sango, and after that, I will be gone from you! *(Getting up, too, and offers Eshu a lobe of kola nut.)* But whatever the case might be; remember that a good friend cannot be bought in the market.

ESHU: *(lobs the lobe into his mouth, then masticating)*. You are right. A good friend cannot be bought in the market. But definitely not a friend like Sango. Have you forgotten after you and I had helped Sango to plunder Ife and Obatala's throne, he mounted afterward; he shook my hand? The last time I saw Sango, he shook my hand. *(Shaking hands with Ogun aggressively.)* That was how Sango shook my hand—the last time I saw him. And you know what that means; when a handshake goes beyond the wrists, it is no longer a handshake but an invitation to wrestling bawl.

OGUN: I know, but—

ESHU: *(cuts in sharply)*. But me no buts, Ogun! I am full of bitterness toward Sango right now, if you must know.

OGUN: To what purpose, exactly, Eshu? Speak, Ogun is anxious!

ESHU: I am bitter because Sango failed to fulfill his promises he made to me when he shook my hand—just the way I shook yours—with a mixture of smile and deceit on his face. Especially, how could he say he would build me a triangular mansion that would surpass my misty oubliette and refuse to do it all these years?

OGUN: *(mumbling surprisingly)*. B-but Sango told me he had already awarded the building contract to Obaluaiye.

ESHU: *(fires up)*. Lies upon lies! Sango did not do anything of such. To be honest, for once, has Sango ever fulfilled any single promise since you and I became his friends?

OGUN: *(heaves a sigh)*. Not that I know of.

ESHU: Ooh o! I am sorry I cannot help him this time. You should know that I am angry with Sango! *(Smashes another gourd on the floor.)*

27

OGUN: I know no doubt! *(Patting Eshu on the shoulder)*. And I must also admit that your grievances were well spelled out, my friend. But no matter how bad a child is, the mother can never allow a wild animal to devour him while she watches. And like I said earlier: a good friend cannot be bought in the market. You have to forgive him... at least for now.

ESHU: *(temper softens)*. All right then. So, when are we going?

OGUN: Nightfall! But we must journey through the savannah. I have some new weapons I need to carry along to put on display. *(Picking up the weapons.)*

ESHU: As I expected.

OGUN: Shall we?

ESHU: We shall!

*[Exeunt.]*

*CURTAIN*

# The Vendetta of the Gods
# Movement Four

*L*angbodo's house. Oyeyemi's continuous groaning is giving Langbodo a serious concern as he evidently walks to and fro trying to idealize a plausible solution to end Oyeyemi's misery and, probably, avert the doomsday.

OYEYEMI: *(groaning intermittently as she keeps calling)* Baba? Baba? *(Now begins to squeeze her breasts in frustration.)* Ah... ah... hmm! Oh no! Baba?

LANGBODO: Oyeyemi... what is it again? *(Attending to her.)* Huh! No, no, no! *(Whirling around and thereby chips in incantations.)* Oyeyemi, a butterfly can only make a sense of taste by the touch of its legs. Oyeyemi, wherever one tree stands, there stands another. But I swear on my father's grave, your perseverance I am yet to fathom... this far! However, I assure you that in no distant time, you shall scale through this endless torture. I promise you this. *(Scooping water from the water pot.)* Oluweri kills, yet whoever brings it, brings life. *(Now sprinkling it on her.)* Softly... softly—either here or there—the snail walks on the earth. Be calm, I say! Aha! Be calm, Oyeyemi! When manhood pours out its slimy content, calmly, it becomes!

*[The water therapy knocks her off into deep sleep. Presently, the three Witches appear masticating human's parts with relish.]*

WITCHES: *(calling in unison).* Langbodo, Oko Ebora inu ogan o! Langbodo, the husband of the anthill!

LANGBODO: *(startles a bit before recognizing the witches).* Ah, ah, ah… the Arometa—the three cooks that never stir a cauldron into pieces.

WITCHES: *(unison).* That is we!

LANGBODO: Indeed!

FIRST WITCH: Well, thanks, but no thanks. *(Thunders.)* Langbodo o! Look at us eyeball to eyeball and tell us how many times your ears heard your name being pronounced forth from our blood-dripping lips?

LANGBODO: Huh! Well, if an alligator that is half deaf could hear the voice of its enemy approaching the swamp, then how much more I, who has a good hearing. Well, Arometa, my name was three times pronounced in one accord.

SECOND WITCH: Hmm! Then, your ears are good—no doubt. But, how come you are so daft lately, eh, Langbodo?

THIRD WITCH: *(bellows).* Langbodo o! Look at me eyeball to eyeball… *(staring at him devilishly)*; how dare you flout our order after the stern warning we gave you last night? We warned you to disassociate yourself from anything that had to do with this woman… here. That was the unanimous instruction from the witches. And if Sango could respect our instruction, we delivered to him through the help of Eshu, then who are you to be rebellious? Langbodo, you betrayed us! Therefore, you are a traitor!

LANGBODO: Traitor? *(shudders.)* Says who?

THIRD WITCH: Says me! What else do you want to hear, huh, Langbodo? *(Now, turning to her fellow Witches.)* So, Eshu was right after all! *(They are nodding their heads in affirmation.)*

FIRST WITCH: Eshu was right after all! *(They are nodding their heads unanimously.)*

SECOND WITCH: Eshu, indeed, he was right after all! *(They continue to nod in one accord, then she bellows again.)* Langbodo…

LANGBODO: *(cuts in angrily).* Enough! Enough of "Eshu this, Eshu that." Awuu! What is it! I must say I am highly disappointed in all of you. You of all people—whose secret of the dead night is at your beck and call—should know what Eshu is capable of doing. Eshu, the confuser of men. The owner of twenty slaves sacrificed all these slaves, one after the other, to appease Eshu so that he would not confuse his head and live peacefully. Yet, Eshu did not spare him more than a night. Eshu confused a newly married wife when she stole from Oya. She said she had not realized that taking two hundred cowries from Oya's shrine was stealing. I can go on and on, to further expose who Eshu is. I am not his fan. In fact, I have never liked him, even when he was trying so hard to be my friend. Because when Eshu tells you to wait for him at this junction, you better go and wait for him at the next junction ahead. The idiot cannot be trusted!

*[Langbodo's monologue has calmed their anger, to the extent that they begin to talk to themselves in silence.]*

WITCHES: *(unison).* Enough! Langbodo? Langbodo?

LANGBODO: That is my name you are calling. *(Chest-thumping.)*

SECOND WITCH: I know. But listen carefully, and if need be, you can call out all the members of your household, here and now, so that they can also hear of this demand we want from you. Well, Langbodo, we the three witches insist that Oyeyemi's blood and that of her unborn baby shall be used for our forthcoming celebration. And mind you, this is not negotiable. We have spoken! *(She laughs while the other two witches join in.)*

LANGBODO: Impossible! I mean, this is not right. Besides, you and I know that we ended that practice long ago at the abyss. We cannot bring back what is dead! No way! I will not allow that. She cannot be used, neither her unborn

31

child! I am sorry to disappoint you! Eshu, or whomever the person is, has no right to dictate who to die or who to survive in my hand. This time, I would not budge whose cow is gored. I am independent of myself. Moreover, the time has passed with the irrevocable of the past if the witches need to be reminded. I think the three of you should leave my house.

FIRST WITCH: Says who?

LANGBODO: You heard me, witch.

FIRST WITCH: *(firing up)*. Insolence! Langbodo, be warned! Do not push us to the wall! It is only a madman that would chase a ram to the wall and not expect the ram to turn back at him fiercely. Do not bite the finger that nurtured your infant head, Langbodo.

LANGBODO: And if I do? Let me say something you witches yet to know about me: I am not afraid of what any of you or your allies can do to the son of Orunmila. I am not your stooge! That I had made clear! Nonsense! I pray, can the three of you kindly leave my house now? It is obvious you have overstayed your time, if you must know!

THIRD WITCH: Huh? All right! We shall go, but be rest assured that we shall return for her blood and that of her child, and you cannot stop us! Let us go!

*[Exeunt.]*

LANGBODO: I see! The sun shall soon set! The sun shall soon set! *(Entering the inner room.)*

*CURTAIN*

# The Vendetta of the Gods
# Movement Five

Sango's palace. Sango enters, who is closely followed by his Royal Bard, who sings his praises. Obatala is chained at stage right; he is smeared with camwood. He groans with pain from Sango's torture. Now, Sango mimics his drunkenness. Obatala is shouting in resistance to a calabash that contains palm wine, which is being forced into his mouth by Sango.

OBATALA: (refusing to drink). No! No! Take the calabash away! Please! It is only a foolish woman that keeps reminding a child where his placenta is buried whenever the child is being violent. I pray you, give me Oluweri—water—instead, to quench my thirst, Sango.

SANGO: (rages). No! (Now smashing a calabash of water on the floor.) A beggar has no choice, Obatala! Have you forgotten? Have you? Well, I hear people singing your praises far and wide: "Obatala, who turns blood into children." Lies upon lies! "Obatala, who created both the good, the bad, and the ugly." That is my problem with you!

OBATALA: But you should not be the one to be angry with me, Sango. Do you know that you are holding me hostage against the will of Eledua and that of the Orishas? Do you?

SANGO: (draws out a sword from its sheath). Swear, Obatala! Swear by this sword that makes a man bleeds to death if you and I did not know what transpired at the abyss of creation… drunkard… that is what you are, Obatala. *(Sits.)*

OBATALA: I beg of you, Sango, please, do not remind me of my ugly past.

ROYAL BARD: *(singing Sango's praises, then thunders).* Sango o!

SANGO: *(rages sharply).* Would you withdraw that wagging tongue of yours at once? Or, else, I will have it cut off and feed it to the dogs. Fool!

*[Entering, Ilesanmi. He appears so agitated.]*

ILESANMI: *(prostrating).* Greetings to Sango—the husband of Oya.

SANGO: Greetings to the wanderer, who wandered into Sango's palace unannounced. Who are you, and what can I do for you?

ILESANMI: *(feigning boldness).* I am Ilesanmi, a farmer from Iranje. I have come to mediate the release of Obatala—the father of laughter.

SANGO: *(laughing).* I see! But do you know that you are a fool? What a wasted odyssey you have embarked on, boy! Oh! Do you think the freedom of Obatala is easy-peasy just like your coconut head that has no content? Indeed, I see! Now listen and listen well. I am not the one holding Obatala hostage. So, go back home. *(Chuckling).*

ILESANMI: Interesting. So, you are telling me right now that you are not the one holding Obatala hostage?

SANGO: *(rages).* Are you saying I am lying?

ILESANMI: I would not dream of that, Sango.

SANGO: You better not, young man. You better not bite more than you can chew by stepping on the tail of a cobra! *(Starts to chew seeds of alligator pepper.)*

ILESANMI: Okay... fine. So, who is responsible for Obatala's imprisonment?

SANGO: Eshu and Ogun.

ILESANMI: Are you sure, Sango?

SANGO: Are you boldly calling me a liar?

ILESANMI: You have not proven otherwise, Sango.

SANGO: Huh! What did you just say?

ILESANMI: You heard me, Sango!

SANGO. Oh, I see! But guess what?

ILESANMI: I do not care whatever you are trying to say if it has nothing to do with the release of Obatala.

SANGO: Then, you are an imbecile... a fool... an idiot, and all that.

SANGO: *(thunders)*. Sango! Sango, in the name of Eledua, release Obatala to me—right now!

SANGO: I have told you I have no hands in Obatala's imprisonment. Perhaps, Eshu and Ogun can explain better whenever you are ready to meet them.

ILESANMI: You can explain better, Sango. So, go ahead!

SANGO: I cannot, and I will not!

ILESANMI: Why, if I may ask?

SANGO: (fires up) Because Eshu and Ogun are demanding for a pound of flesh, each, from Obatala for the sacrilegious act he had committed in the time past. Now, take my advice: go, or wander back to wherever you came from and continue your farming. But about your demand to release Obatala to you, that is dead on arrival. So, go back home, stranger!

ILESANMI: Never! You cannot make a woman out of me, Sango! I do not care about what anybody says; I will confront Ogun and Eshu and then free the father of laughter. Obatala shall be free today, Sango!

SANGO: *(cautioning).* You better be careful what you wish for, son.

ILESANMI: I am not your son, Sango! I can never be your son! Sango, do you know the son of whom I am? *(Now carrying himself in a gait manner.)*

SANGO:*(chuckles).* Whoever the son of whom you are, he does not ring a bell. Look here, stranger, I may be patient like a dove; but when I am vexed, my venomous fang is deadly. Now, run along!

ILESANMI: I said not until Obatala is released and come home with me, Sango.

SANGO: You are a fool! I am sure it must be the wisdom of that traitor, Orunmila, that is sustaining you from committing suicide thus far. How dare you seek a battleground with Eshu Odara, who hits his head against a stone till that stone starts bleeding, when he is angry? Or Ogun, the god of war, who has water in his pots but prefers to bath with blood? I think you are drunk on the same palm wine Obatala drank at the abyss of creation. Because I have not seen where someone will be digging his own grave, and then buries himself afterward.

*[ILESANMI becomes angry as he glances at the moon, which is about to become fully round.]*

ILESANMI: *(brings out a talisman).* I swear by the manhood of Obatala, I will fight Eshu and Ogun, or anybody, to a standstill today.

SANGO: *(fires up)* But remember that a fly that refuses to part ways with a stinking corpse before being lowered into the grave will follow the corpse to the world beyond. When a child keeps asking about what killed his father from his wicked uncle, he is unknowingly asking for the same death that killed his father.

ILESANMI: Do not play games with me, Sango!

SANGO: I do not play games; in fact, I am too old for that now! Well, I think I have enjoyed enough display of your madness. So, stop dilly-dallying around and go home. Otherwise, your skull will be used for drinking wine!

ILESANMI: I will be the first to use your skull to drink wine, Sango!

SANGO: Be careful, young man! Be careful! Because a child who says when he is old, he will use the head of a certain bird to eat; the birds will never pray well for such child to grow old to fulfill his promise! Madman, be warned! Do not be like that little bird, who bumped into a sumptuous meal and after having his fill, then challenged his Chi to a wrestling match.

ILESANMI: There is nothing a burning fire can do to the back of a tortoise, Sango!

SANGO: When a child suddenly becomes so bold to challenge an old man, it lives everybody with two assumptions: either the child has become so rich overnight, or he has some kind of spiritual forces backing him. I, therefore, ask: who is bankrolling you?

ILESANMI: I do not care about your insubordination, Sango, but I will not leave your palace without Obatala. So, do your worst!

SANGO: How dare you challenge me?! I, Sango, a god after Eledumare!

ILESANMI: You cannot scare me with your raves, Sango!

SANGO: *(thunders)*. Leave my palace and go home to your dying wife, young man!

ILESANMI: Sango… *(Sobbing.)* Those who have their palm kernel cracked for them by Eshu, Ogun, even by a benevolent spirit, should not mock the misfortune of others.

SANGO: Come on, get out of my sight! What insolense! Nonsense!

*[Ilesanmi brandishes his sword. Presently, enter, Eshu and Ogun.]*

SANGO: *(getting up to welcome them)*. Ah! Ah! Eshu… Ogun. *(They embrace.)* It has been donkey's years the vulture met her death at the hand of Orunmila worshipers at Ogbomosho. Eshu… Ogun, I am glad both of you came. What an august visit! I hope I am safe?

OGUN: Of course, you are not. *(Laughing deliriously.)*

SANGO: You got jokes, brother. *(Giggles, then turns to Eshu.)* Aha! How have you been, my friend?

ESHU: *(wriggling his nose here and there)*. What do you think?

SANGO: *(he understands the anger in Eshu's voice)*. I understand. Well, I am sorry, my good friend. I promise I will make it up to you. Please?

ESHU: If you say so! But you know me too well, Sango, that no matter how angry I am towards you, I can never plot your downfall. The oat that binds us together is irrevocable, my friend.

SANGO: That is the spirit! By the way, I must say, I am happy for honoring my invitation about this war that is drumming so hard to crumble my kingdom.

ESHU: When Ogun told me about it, I was angry, but I had to be reminded by Ogun when he said, "A good friend cannot be bought in the market."

OGUN: That was exactly what I told him, Sango.

SANGO: Thank you, Ogun. You have done well!

OGUN: What are friends for, Sango? My loyalty to you can never be broken! Sango, I greet you!

SANGO: Ogun, I greet you, too, for mediating between Eshu and me. Indeed, you are a peacemaker! *(Thunders.)* Ogun o!

OGUN: *(thunders in response).* Sango o! *(Now, calling.)* Sango?

SANGO: *(self-adulation).* It is a god you are calling, my friend.

OGUN: Sango, who rides fire like a horse. Sango, who is always impatient, like a woman on her menstrual flow. Sango, the man who keeps the drunken Obatala hostage without anyone dares to ask him. Indeed, it has been ages, my good friend. Nonetheless, I am happy to honor this invitation and go on this battle, fighting side-by-side with you and Eshu. *(Sango and Ogun headbutt each other.)*

ESHU: Make way, Ogun, let me also eulogize my lone friend, Sango. *(Moving closer to Sango—side-by-side.)* Sango, husband of Oya, who stole from a farm, and the owner of the farm called out to passersby to come and catch the thief. But when the passerby came, the farmer said he was the thief, while Sango was the owner of the farm. *(Chuckles.)*

SANGO: *(self-adulation).* That is me! Sometimes, I look at myself and say, "Sango, you are too wicked!" *(Laughs.)* Eshu, you know me, and you are doing well!

ESHU: Sango, husband of Osun, who knows that when I am vexed, I will hit my head on a stone until that stone becomes gush with blood; I greet you.

SANGO: *(chuckles).* Let me entertain both of you. *(He rolls out a drum.)* The "hide" on this drum is a new one; in fact, it is like a virgin boy who has never been defiled by a woman. *(Chuckling.)*

*[Eshu and Ogun dance to the rhythmic batá drum as Sango hits on. Meanwhile, Ilesanmi is watching closely. Soon, they stop. Now, panting.]*

SANGO: That is the spirit! Once again, you are welcome brothers... My house is your house. So, be comfortable.

*[Sango gives them seat,s but Eshu prefers to sit on the bare floor.]*

OGUN: *(drops his weapons, then suddenly notices Ilesanmi).* So, Sango, you have not stopped your rascality after all? Now, tell me, when did you capture this rhesus monkey? *(Pointing at Ilesanmi.)*

SANGO: *(acting surprised).* So, you are still here? *(To Ogun.)* Well, the monkey, as you rightfully addressed him, has come boldly to demand the release of Obatala. And, besides, he has sworn to fight—

ESHU: *(cuts in).* Fight? And if I may ask, with who, Sango? *(Immediately, he begins to roll up his sleeves in preparation for a fight.)*

SANGO: You and Ogun, of course. He said he would kill everybody and destroy my palace unless we released Obatala to him—unscathed. But I told him that his foolishness could be likened to the proverbial mouse that challenged the cat for a fight after it had already become drunk on the same cat's urine.

OGUN: I see! What a fine choice! *(Picking two swords: he tosses one to Eshu, now brandishing.)*

OBATALA: *(from where is being tied up).* This is a travesty, Sango! Run, Ilesanmi! Run for your life!

ILESANMI: I will go… but I shall return for your heads! *(Running off.)*

OGUN: Poor thing. Pity! *(Now facing Eshu.)* He should have waited for my combat extravagances. Nonsense!

SANGO: Can a dog challenge a lion? *(They collectively burst into laughter.)*

*CURTAIN*

# The Vendetta of the Gods
## Movement Six

*Sango's secret hut. Ogunde (a medicine man) is preparing Sango for more fortification. In the meantime, Sango keeps on pounding the substances in a mortar, obviously, bare-chested. Ogunde, throws a live chick in the mortar while Sango relishes the pounding.*

OGUNDE: *(thunders Sango's name continuously)*. Sango o? Sango o? Sango o?

SANGO: *(thunders in response)*. Eeh o! *(Whirling, and then continues his pounding.)*

OGUNDE: Sango, look at me eyeball to eyeball and tell me how many times did I call your name?

SANGO: The great one, I am not deaf—like the crocodile—that I would not hear that my name was echoed three times, or blind, am I, like the bat, that I would not see that your lips reverberated three times while calling the fire-breathing god.

OGUNDE: That is the spirit! *(Laughs.)* But, Sango, do you know what you are pounding so vigorously that your testicles throw caution to the wind as they keep swinging beneath your thighs?

SANGO: I would not know, the great one. But I think they are somewhat combinations of leaves... black soap... just like that.

OGUNDE: *(sighs)*. Hmm!

SANGO: Your silence speak volume, great one!

*[Ogunde laughs vehemently as he throws another substance into the mortar.]*

OGUNDE: *(incantation)*. Well. A child who does not know the potency of a charm calls it mere leaves. However, bits and pieces of this and that make it whole—a potency of a charm. *(Laughing broadly.)* Sango, it is the time! So, give the pestle a break!

*[Ogunde begins to lacerate Sango's body with a sharp object and then applies the substance on the bleeding spots.]*

OGUNDE: *(smacks Sango three times on the back)*. Aha! Aha! Aha! *(Thunders Sango's name.)* Sango o! Whoever waits for you for a fight, waits for his death! Sango traveled to Ede and arrived at Ilorin!

SANGO: *(cuts in mumbling)*. B-but I thought I arrived at Ogbomosho, the great one?

OGUNDE: Of course, you did not! It was Ilorin; in fact, it was the village of Ikukoyi—the great medicine man of his time and whom you killed while making sweet love to his wife.

SANGO: That was a simple navigation error, old man.

OGUNDE: And when did Sango start to care about a simple navigation error? The Sango I know does not have a good knowledge of the four cardinal points; hence he does not care about surveying his enemies like a vulture would a piece of a carcass before he pounces on them.

SANGO: Of course, you are right, the great one. I do not map before I set out to execute. I do not look before I leap like a frog. *(Smacks his lips.)* I hate myself for this! But in fact, I do enjoy it. *(Laughing cynically.)*

OGUNDE: *(sighs sharply.)* Well, Sango, the ritual is done. And I can practically tell you that no one born from the womanliness of a woman can have you killed. But I tell you of this: never leave your enemies behind; otherwise, they will come, rise against your throat, and demand for your head. My part is done here, Sango. Do you have anything to say?

SANGO: Yes, I do, the great one!

OGUNDE: Go ahead, Kabieyesi!

SANGO: *(clears his throat, then calls)*. The great one?

OGUNDE: I can hear you, Kabieyesi.

SANGO: Do you know I am heretofore to understand why I have been worried lately? I mean, I have been thinking, even more than a god should, how these wars I have been fighting lately came about in the first place. I can tell you I did not draw the first blood of any of these wars. Neither did I call for any of it, for me to strengthen my kingdom, nor did I become so power-drunk that I wanted to eliminate all mankind from the surface of the earth. Is there something somebody is not telling me, the great one?

OGUNDE: *(sighs deeply)*. I do not know anything, Kabieyesi. Maybe you should consult an Ifa oracle. Who knows? You may find the answer you are looking for. Kabieyesi, the insect that eats up a vegetable stays beneath the vegetable. Kabieyesi, it is the mouse that lives in the house that tells the one in the wood that there is plenty of food in the house. I do not think you hear me, Kabieyesi?

SANGO: I do, the great one. Well, it might not be as exactly as how you wanted me to, but I can assure you that there is no smoke without a fire.

OGUNDE: That is my point exactly!

SANGO: Aha! One more thing.

OGUNDE: Proceed, Kabieyesi. I am all ears!

SANGO: My father once said to me that "if you are alive and you do not get feedback about yourself, does that not mean you are a dead man walking? If that is not it, then I do not know what else to call it." So, I am sure you aware of the rumor flying around town lately?

OGUNDE: You mean the rumor about how tyrannically you have been ruling Ife? Or the one about how you are intending to increase tax level on both the employed and unemployed respectively?

SANGO: All of the above!

OGUNDE: I see!

SANGO: *(sharply)*. What did you see, exactly?

OGUNDE: Argh, Kabieyesi!

SANGO: I mean, who do people say I am? At least I am not all that bad!?

OGUNDE: *(exclaims surprisingly)*. Aah, Kabieyesi! At times, we should damn the consequences by telling the truth!

SANGO: *(slightly anxious)*. Okay!?

OGUNDE: *(coaxed gently as he speaks)*. Kabieyesi, let us be truthful to ourselves for once. You and I know that when a god forces his way into power and begins to reign supreme—after tasting the sweetness of power and luxury—he will eventually lose his godhead and then becomes an ordinary man.

SANGO: *(cold expression of suspicious motive registers on his face)*. I see! So, what is the point exactly?

OGUNDE: As I suggested earlier, Kabieyesi, you must visit an Ifa Oracle priest who can help you to right many of your wrongs. I must confess, you have too many wrongs, Kabieyesi!

SANGO: I know! I am a huge failure, right?

OGUNDE: *(refutes sharply)*. I did not say so, Kabieyesi.

SANGO: I see! *(suddenly remembers something.)* Aha! I just know exactly what I have to do.

OGUNDE: And what could that be, Kabieyesi?

SANGO: I am thinking I should go to Arubidi to visit the figurine of Oranmiyan—my father.

OGUNDE: Hmm! That is a great idea, Kabieyesi. Meanwhile, I have to take my leave. *(Now he begins to dance to the rhythmic batá drum of Sango.)*

SANGO: Impressive. By nature, you deserve a parting embrace, the great one.

*[Sango rises and moves closer to Ogunde; he hugs him and stabs him in the stomach. Sharply, he turns to the audience to caution them.]*

SANGO: Confidently, I speak to caution all, and sundry, please, do not spare the lives of those who know the secrete source of your power in any circumstances. Otherwise, they will come back in the dead of night, stripe you off before they cut off your head! *(Laughs cynically.)*

ROYAL BARD: *(from afar, he thunders)*. Sango o! I pray, please do not let me meet my death in your hand someday. *(Thunders again.)* Sango o! Two seasons ago, I told a palm wine tapper from Ijesha that whoever waited for Sango for a fight, waited for his death. But the man doubted me of what you are capable of doing, especially when you are vexed, my lord.

SANGO: *(cuts in keenly)*. The fool doubted you? Wait a minute… is there still a single soul left in that eh… Ilesha?

ROYAL BARD: It is Ijesha, my lord.

SANGO: Whatever! So, there is still a single soul dwelling in Ijesha after the genocide I instructed Gbonka to carry out? *(Grabbing Royal Bard by the throat, but suddenly restrains.)*

ROYAL BARD: *(breathing heavily)*. My lord, there are thousands of villagers living in Ijesha as I speak to you right now. Besides, business is booming for them. But come to think of it, my lord, Sango, did you think Gbonka, in his foolishness, would carry out a genocide in the village his beloved mother comes from? I am afraid to say Gbonka would do no such thing. I do not think you understand me, my lord?

SANGO: *(moving to and fro as he bits his finger in frustration)*. So, Gbonka fooled me after all… me, Sango! I see! Well! Now, can you finish telling me about the palm wine tapper who you said he doubted you?

ROYAL BARD: *(acting surprised)*. Oh, the fool died, my lord! I mean, in my own very eyes he was struck dead by your thunderous hand immediately when he doubted me.

SANGO: *(laughing broadly, now self-adulation)*. I am Sango; sometimes I kill without my knowledge. Then I say: whoever engages an elephant in a battle demands for his death unknowingly.

ROYAL BARD: Sango took over a wealthy man's house at Ede and then downgraded him from being a landlord to a common cleaner.

SANGO: That is one out of many things I am capable of doing—quintessentially. *(laughing broadly, and then falls asleep on a mat while the Royal Bard exits.)*

*[Presently, the Three Witches enter. Meanwhile, Sango is deeply snoring.]*

WITCHES: *(in unison, they thunder)*. Sango o!

*[Sango startles up, then quickly picks a sword in preparation for a fight.]*

SANGO: *(Now, he recognizes them)*. Ah, ah… the Arometa?

WITCHES: *(in unison)*. It is we, the Arometa, who never stir a cauldron into pieces, Sango. *(They flirt their bloody fingers.)*

SANGO: That is the spirit! *(Sharply pointing the sword at them.)* Now let me get something straight: were the three of you trying to kill me in my sleep a few minutes ago?

SECOND WITCH: We dare not, Sango. A dog may be ravenous, but that does not make it eats its kind.

FIRST WITCH: Sango, have you forgotten that whoever waits to engage you in a fight waits for his death?

SANGO: That is me—it has become a ritual of me. *(Now carrying himself in a gait manner and then sits.)* By the way, to what purpose do I own this august visit? Speak, Sango is all ears!

THIRD WITCH: Sango, have you not noticed lately that the sacrifices at the Idi Iroko are no longer there and the ritual by the mortals has also stopped?

SANGO: Did anybody say it was Sango who ate the sacrifices at the Idi Iroko? Or did anybody say it was Sango who killed those people that were bringing those sacrifices to the Idi Iroko? Or should I say something stupidly is wrong with your kingdom?

WITCHES: *(they attack Sango fiercely)*. Blasphemy, Sango!

THIRD WITCH: *(charging towards Sango fiercely)*. Sango? Sango? Sango?

SANGO: *(raging)*. What is it? Did you forget it was a god you were calling, witch?

THIRD WITCH: I did not. *(Staring closely at Sango's eyes)*. But how many times did your name come out of my venomous tongue, Sango?

SANGO: *(stepping backward boldly)*. Oh, oh, wait a minute, would your three times calling "Sango" should make me shudder like a feverish hen? *(Feigning trembling.)* Never! I, Sango, who spits fire like a dragon—a fire-breathing monster—cannot be frightened by anything. When I kill, nobody dares to ask. Because no man dines and wines with death and live to tell the beautiful story.

FIRST WITCH: Spare me your raves, Sango. It seems you have forgotten so soon that we were the ones that nursed and doctored your infant head at the transitional gulf. So, I am afraid. Because absolute power has made you forget so soon that we were the one that helped you to overthrow Obatala and other gods—far and wide—especially the throne you are mounting today, was made possible because of the assist we rendered you, Sango.

SANGO: *(rages, then walks a few steps around)*. Enough! Nobody has ever helped Sango—without their selfish interest at the fore—in his horrendous enterprise, neither now nor in the time passed. As a matter of fact, those who volunteer to help Sango—advertently or inadvertently—deserve no appreciation in return. I pray we are done here. *(Returning to his seat.)*

SECOND WITCH: *(sighs sharply)*. Well, Sango, they say two wrongs cannot make a right. Now, can you kindly fulfill your part of the bargain, and we will be out of your misty shrine. I mean, all we demanded of you were just seven humans: three male and four females—that was our bargain, Sango.

SANGO: *(rises again)*. But I am afraid to say that none of you do deserve a single human sacrifice, let alone the numbers you mentioned. Now, please leave my house. Otherwise, the three of you will regret ever coming in the first place. Or have you forgotten that I am a god of short fuss?

FIRST WITCH: I do not care, Sango, but do not break the oath!

SANGO: And if I do, what would the three of you do to me? *(Laughing, then suddenly restrains.)* Look! I only take part in an oath just to break them. Perhaps you should ask Ogun, or better still, ask your friend, Eshu Odara; he will gladly tell you the man behind this mask. *(Pointing a finger right back at his face and then laughs broadly.)*

THIRD WITCH: I am so disappointed in you, Sango. In fact, you are an ingrate! And Sango, for betraying us, you...

WITCHES: *(in unison)*. You will suffer and beg Death to take your life! It is so!

THIRD WITCH: We have spoken!

*[Sango begins to search for his gun frantically. Meanwhile, the witches scoop a live chicken that is being tied down and then leave in a hurry.]*

SANGO: *(now, he fetches out a gun)*. They should have waited for me to test this new gun I bought from Ogun on them. *(Corking the gun.)* Nonsense! *(Now, he notices the chicken is missing, chuckles.)* Oh, they eat that, too? Scavengers! *(Laughing as he drops the gun.)*

ROYAL BARD: *(thunders)*. Sango o! *(Eulogizing.)* Sango, husband of Oya o! May your reign be peaceful like the mind of a woman who enjoys the manhood of her husband alone and shades it from the prying eyes of other women! May Oduduwa extend his blessings towards you, Kabeiyesi!

SANGO: *(rubbing his palms together solemnly)* It is so! *(Laughs.)* I think your sweet tongue deserves a penny... Come with me.

*[Exeunt.]*

*CURTAIN*

# The Vendetta of the Gods
# Movement Seven

*L*angbodo's house. Langbodo is casting his Opele Oracle. He seems frustrated. *Meanwhile, Oyeyemi continues to groan in pain.*

LANGBODO: *(casting Opele Oracle, now soliloquizing).* In the creation year, when Obatala was singled out to lead the creation process, Orunmila was perplexed. However, in the year followed and to date, Sango says he prefers war to peace. Then I ask: who will now settle the quarrel between the father of peace and the father of war? Hmm! Pity!

*[Ilesanmi enters wearily from the entrance and then looks at the moon on the wall].*

ILESANMI: *(calling).* Baba? Baba?

LANGBODO: *(turns sharply to attend to him).* Gods of our land! Horror! What happened to you? *(shaking him vigorously.)* Be a man and speak, Ilesanmi!

ILESANMI: I was attacked by Sango and his rascals: Ogun and Eshu.

LANGBODO: *(reprimanding Ilesanmi's action).* Oh, no! You should not have gone there in the first place. Gods of our land! Children of nowadays and their rashness! So, what transpired?

ILESANMI: *(standing erect)*. Baba… when I got to Sango's palace, I met him; he was sitting on this throne like a proud peacock, and then I politely asked him to release Obatala to me, but he refused point blank on the premises that he was not the one holding Obatala hostage but Eshu and Ogun. *(Blowing his watery nostril.)*

LANGBODO: Lies upon lies! Sango tells lies more than a lawyer. The Oracle cannot be false!

ILESANMI: However, I told him that I would challenge whosoever that was holding Obatala hostage. But lo and behold, when I saw the arrival of Eshu and Ogun…it was like the arrival of over four hundred gods of Ife kingdom. I must confess, when I saw the fire burning in the eyes of Eshu and Ogun, I suddenly became a walking dead like one of those we see in the evil forest. Baba, I was terrified! And as I speak right now, my body aches—especially my head.

LANGBODO: *(laughing)*. Ha, ha!

ILESANMI: *(rubbing his sore head)*. You think it is funny, huh? Well, you have to do something quickly before ache kills me. *(Propping his chin up.)*

*[Langbodo picks a substance and rubs it on Ilesanmi's head to ease the pain.]*

LANGBODO: Eshu has done what he knows how to do best, Ilesanmi. Eshu, who prefers to go to the markets to throws stones simply because he does not care whether his mother is in the market or not. Let me tell you a story. A long time ago, when tigers used to smoke, Eshu embarked on a disastrous journey to Osogbo. He was going to visit a particular man who lived in a glasshouse to learn about the trick of how to throw a stone today and hit the head of a victim the following day. Luckily, Eshu was taught all the tricks, and he was happy. But before he left Osogbo that fateful day, he threw four hundred stones on the roofs of many houses, including that of the man who taught him the trick. And when Ogun was trying to reprimand him for his bad action, he shut Ogun up and then said in the craftiest manner: "If you will stop the sales of your weapons, Ogun, I, Eshu, might also stop inciting trouble. What do you think?" That condition was too much for Ogun to consider, so he told Eshu to master his trick. And to date, Eshu has continued to incite trouble everywhere he goes, believing that when he finally masters his trick, he would probably stop.

ILESANMI: I will stop him before he achieves his evil aim.

LANGBODO: *(grunts)*. Listen to me. You cannot fight what is beyond you, son. Especially, when you have not completed the necessary rite that will aid you to defeat Sango and his allies. You have to be patient! Because it takes patience to await a stammerer to finish pronouncing the word "abracadabra." So, what else happened?

ILESANMI: *(readily)*. As I was saying, I saw a jaw-dropping scenario. Baba? I mean, with my own very eyes, I saw Eshu and Ogun dancing to the rhythmic batá drum of Sango instead of the sixteen Igbim drums of Obatala. Why? Join me, Baba.

*[The drums cue them in to mimic the dance of Eshu and Ogun. The steps pulsate the rhythm of the drum. They stop dancing as each breaks a sweat.]*

ILESANMI: Baba, for how long will a feverish dog tremble before her keeper takes her to a vet? Oh, it is unfair, Baba! *(Collecting the wine Langbodo offers him.)* That reminds me. Why is Obatala being referred to as drunk? And why does Sango, in conjunction with his rascals, want a pound of flesh from Obatala? *(Cleaning his sweaty face intermittently with his soaking shirt.)*

LANGBODO: I think it is time I told you the story. Although, it was a long story. *(Sighs sharply.)* The vendetta of the gods started a long time ago at the abyss of creation; and even before the vulture was created to pacify a waring god, Eledumare—the creator—gave Obatala the mandate to create every mortal despite the displeasure put forward by other gods, chiefly by Sango, Ogun, and Eshu. In the long run, something tragic happened, which birthed the animosity the gods have for one another to date.

ILESANMI: Was Eledumare regretted of his fine choice?

LANGBODO: Not really. Well, the task of creation was an enviable one, and every other god was equally interested to champion the cause. So, the conspiracy and the envy were greatly tailored out against Obatala. It is pertinent to know that Obatala was bewitched at the eve of creation by Egbere—a diminutive gnome—who transformed into a beautiful woman and then seduced him to get drunk—he became so drunk in love and on palm wine on the eve of creation. Can you imagine? As a drunk, he was, he began to carry out the task of creation entrusted to him by Eledumare. Consequently, the blinds, the albinos, and the hunchbacks were the aftermaths of his drunkenness. Pity, why not! *(Picks up kola nut from a bowl, then starts masticating it.)*

ILESANMI: Was there no remedy? *(Also, he removes a kola nut, throws a lobe into his mouth, and starts masticating with relish.)*

LANGBODO: There was a vulture. The vulture that carried the sacrifice that was meant to pacify the anger of the gods was later killed by the sons of Orunmila at Oshogbo; however, it was a simple cause of navigation error. This singular act of mistake arouses the anger of the gods beyond the limit, hence they sent Sango to displace Obatala from his palace in Ife. Pity, why not!

ILESANMI: And imprisoned him?

LANGBODO: That is where the demand for a pound of flesh comes into play. *(Laughs broadly.)*

ILESANMI: So, how can the gods be pacified? I mean, there should be a messiah, eh, Baba?

LANGBODO: *(sighs calmly)*. Hmm! Aha! Okitika. How time flies! *(Picking another lobe of kola nut.)*

ILESANMI: *(impatiently)*. Who is Okitika? And can he be of help, Baba?

LANGBODO: *(uncertainty)*. Yes. I mean, no. Well, he was a man from Ugbo who was Sango's loyal servant. No. I mean, loyal friend. But unfortunately, he met his death in between the thighs of a princess at Okitipupa—a town that was later named after him. He was the only one who could dare to withstand the burning eyes of Sango in the time passed.

ILESANMI: Too bad! Nevertheless, I will confront Sango, Eshu, Ogun, and release Obatala. *(Clinching his fist in anger)*. I swear by the manhood of Obatala!

LANGBODO: Ilesanmi? When crocodiles eat their eggs, what will they not do to the flesh of a frog?

ILESANMI: That was a proverb. I hate proverbs! So, forgive me if I cannot make head or tail of your words, Baba.

LANGBODO: I see! Well, Sango is a man, who does not know either friends or foes when he is angry. If Sango could send Gbonka to Ede to have Timi beheaded, and then had Gbonka to suffer the full weights of his anger—both who were his soldiers—what will he not do to a mere mortal like you, eh, Ilesanmi?

ILESANMI: I am not a coward, Baba. I will fight Sango and his rascals to a standstill and then bring Obatala home to his people. *(Now brandishing a sword.)*

LANGBODO: Son, too many words do not fill a basket. So, relax.

*[Oyeyemi starts to groan in pain, and they rush to attend to her.]*

LANGBODO: Ilesanmi, go and seek help… Go now!

ILESANMI: Where shall I find help… where, Baba? Please, help me! *(Moving to and fro, now seeking help from the audience who are in turn lost in between the web of the situation.)*

AUDIENCE: *(in unison)*. We understand how you feel, arakurin—young fellow—but we are helpless, too. We are sorry!

ILESANMI: *(crutches beneath the floor sobbing uncontrollably)*. Argh! Whaa-whaa!

LANGBODO: *(pouring libation, now, calling)*. Ilesanmi?

ILESANMI: *(beaming with tears)*. Y-yes, Baba...

LANGBODO: *(staring at a mirror keenly)*. The Oracle is saying you shall go to Owu. And when you get into the town, find someone to show you the compound of Oluode, then ask about Akala, the blind bat; he will give you a substance that will help you.

ILESANMI: *(gets up sharply)*. Is that all? *(Sniffing.)*

LANGBODO: *(coughs)*. As soon as Akala gives you the substance, leave his house at once and find a way to get to Oya and give her the substance; you will see what happens next. *(Rising gently.)* No matter how small a grain of salt is, an earthworm cannot rub it on its body. The penis does not have eyes, but when it becomes erect like a straight rod, it will locate the vagina with ease. Obatala must be released for the sake of procreation—for a continuance of the rite of passage.

*[Langbodo, immediately, turns at the sound of Oyeyemi's groaning, and then turns to Ilesanmi.]*

LANGBODO: And Oyeyemi must not die! Now, go! Go, Ilesanmi! *(Quivering an iron staff.)*

*[Ilesanmi goes to give his wife a kiss on the forehead amidst tears and then exits.]*

*CURTAIN*

# The Vendetta of the Gods
# Movement Eight

*A*kalas's shrine. *The curtain opens to reveal a misty shrine, and Eshu and Ogun are sitting opposite each other, patiently waiting for Akala to attend to them. Suddenly, Eshu farts; Ogun becomes uncomfortable with the smell. He covers his nose from inhaling the smell.*

OGUN: *(freeing his palm to breathe fresh air, then clears his throat).* As I was about to ask before your fart almost choked me to death, when was the last time you visited the market behind your oubliette?

ESHU: I cannot remember. I stopped going to that market since the day they conspired against me that I was the one flaming the amber of commotion among the marketers.

OGUN: Well, the way the market is booming right now; it will give you a jaw-dropping surprise, Eshu. As I speak to you right now, I have a large store full of merchandise in that market, my friend.

ESHU: You are not serious?

OGUN: Come on, has your bitterness toward Sango now made you start doubting your childhood friend?

ESHU: And you think what Sango is doing is not enough reason for one to start doubting his father—let alone his friends?

OGUN: But did I not tell you that I would build myself an empire of business someday? *(Laughing deliriously.)*

ESHU: Well, my friend, you must forgive me for not leaping for joy because I cannot remember if you ever told me so. Nevertheless, congratulations! *(Chucking cynically.)*

OGUN: That is the spirit! *(Continues laughing.)*

ESHU: I am so proud of you, Ogun. *(Shaking Ogun's hand a couple of times.)*

OGUN: I am also proud of you, too, Eshu. *(Smiling.)*

ESHU: Of course, you should! *(Now disengages his hand from Ogun's Well, not so happy.)*

[*Presently, Akala emerges from the back door and then sits. He howls to elicit fear and horror. Now, he strikes a gong three times.*]

AKALA: *(he clears his throat)*. The spirit world says I should greet both of you for your patience!

OGUN AND ESHU: *(unison)*. Tell them their greetings were well received, the great one. *(They laugh.)*

OGUN: *(sharply)*. Make way, Eshu, let me greet the old wizard! Aha! Greetings to Akala, the blind bat who sees the unknown!

ESHU: *(sharply as he thunders)*. Akala o! The bat may be dangling upside-down, but that does not mean it cannot see the eagle in the sky. Akala, the blind bat… who sees more than those who have two eyes, I greet you, the great one.

AKALA: That is the spirit! *(Incantation.)* A man who does not know where the rain began to drench him will not remember when the sun started to dry his body. When a child is in trouble, he will run from his father to the bosom of his mother for help. The snail says if the tortoise cannot run faster, he should leave the way for him to take a lead. Our people say, "A rabbit does not journey in daylight for nothing." So, what could that thing be, which made both of you visit Akala unannounced?

OGUN AND ESHU: *(unison)*. A disturbing one, the great one.

AKALA: *(grunts in a guttural voice as he turns to Ogun)*. Hmm! Well, let me see your palm.

OGUN: *(contemplating)*. Which hand, the great one?

AKALA: Your mother's hand, Ogun. *(bites a kola nut, then starts masticating.)*

OGUN: *(opens his left palm)*. There you go, the great one.

AKALA: *(sprinkling a whitish substance on it)*. Fold your palm... more tightly, then whisper into it solemnly whatever the reason that brought you here, and when you are done, mention your mother's name three times.

*[Ogun begins to whisper solemnly. Meanwhile, Akala gives Eshu a lobe of kola nut to eat.]*

OGUN: *(after he finishes, he presents his palm)*. There you go, the great one!

AKALA: *(staring closely at the palm, then spites into it)*. What I see here... I mean, what your palm reads, is so clear to me. It says you want a powerful charm that can cast spell on Sango, to cause more trouble and wars for himself, and the reason is that you want to keep selling more weapons and your business to keep booming. Am I right?

OGUN: That is correct, the great one!

AKALA: Then consider it done, Ogun, son of Yemaya! Take this... *(Gives Ogun a substance.)* Every morning, sprinkle it in your shrine for seven market days and seven market days after that. That is all. Leave the rest thing to me. *(Laughing cynically.)*

OGUN: Thank you, the great one! *(Now, he puts the substance into his bag amidst cynical laughter.)*

*[Akala turns and gestures at Eshu to open his left palm. Eshu obeys. Akala sprinkles a whitish substance on it and then asks him to fold it before whispering whatever reason that brings him.]*

ESHU: *(whispers solemnly).* There you go, the great one!

AKALA: *(staring closely at the open palm, then spits on it).* Did you remember mentioning your mother's name three times?

ESHU: Yes, I did, the great one.

AKALA: That is the spirit! *(Begins to strike a metal gong three times, then thunders).* Eshu o!

ESHU: *(responding thunderously).* Eeh o!

AKALA: Eshu, the great opportunist and all-seeing god, all-hearing gate-keeper of the crossroads, I greet you.

ESHU: I greet you, too, the great one!

AKALA: But Eshu, what you want me to do for you is a bit difficult; nevertheless, I will see what I can do, but it is going to cost you a lot.

ESHU: Name your price, the great one; I, Eshu... *(boasting)*, I am equal to any task—name your price.

AKALA: Ha, ha! I am a believer in what you are capable of, Eshu. But if you want Sango to pay dearly for his lies and betrayal toward you, then you have to come back here next market day—and it has to be in the night. Remember, the secrete of a night owl should not be revealed to the other birds in broad daylight. *(Laughing cynically.)* I do not think you understand me? Do you?

ESHU: I do, the great one!

AKALA: It is better that way, Eshu. You see, I cannot give you what will not work for you. I do not think you understand me? Do you?

ESHU: I perfectly understand you, the great one! It is just that I cannot wait to see Sango go through pains and agony and then offer him a basket to cry a river of tears in it and force him to drink therefrom. *(Now, losing his temper.)* How could Sango lie to me the third time that he would build me a triangular mansion that would surpass my oubliette and did not do it afterward?

OGUN: I wonder!

ESHU: I am not stupid, the great one! The hunter thinks the monkey is not wise; it is because he forgets that the monkey has its logic.

AKALA: That is my point exactly. Listen, a corpse can never hide from those who will bury it. I do not think you understand me?

ESHU: I cannot doubt you, even when I am not sober, the great one!

AKALA: That is the spirit!

OGUN: *(cuts in worrying)*. It is getting dark, the great one. So, I think we should be on our way now. Besides, I need to pick a few things as we journey back home—through the savannah.

AKALA: It is all right! *(Pouring libation)*. May Eledua—the creator—make your journey back home a smooth one! *(Hitting a metal gong three times.)*

OGUN AND ESHU: *(affirming in unison)*. Ase! It is so! Thank you, the great one!

*[Ogun and Eshu spring up; they headbutt each other before heading to the exit door. Meanwhile, Ilesanmi enters but ducks immediately when he sees Ogun and Eshu coming out of Akala's shrine. He is dumbfounded.]*

*CURTAIN*

# The Vendetta of the Gods
# Movement Nine

*ango's palace. Sango mounts his throne. He is flanked at the ride side by Ogun and at the left side by Eshu, respectively. Each of them holds a calabash of wine, mimicking Obatala amidst laughter. Obatala is still chained at the right side of the stage.*

OBATALA: *(self-adulation)*. I am Obatala, the god who turns blood into children. Sango, have you not tortured me enough without adding such an eyesore to it? *(He closes his eyes.)*

ESHU: *(teasing Obatala)*. This is how you were drunk on the eve of creation. *(Drinking more as some drips out of his mouth.)* Obatala, posterity will judge you on drunkenness!

OBATALA: No Sango! You are the one posterity shall judge.

SANGO: Lies upon lies! *(Gulping more palm wine, then returns to Obatala)* The ample time I gave you is running out like a man with a low sperm count, so when do you want to kick the bucket?

OBATALA: *(pleading)*. Sango, I beg of you, please, take these chains off me so I can go and appease the ancestral spirit of the unborn. Besides, you and I know that the world is transient, and no one can alter it! *(Thunders.)* Now, do the needful, Sango!

ESHU: Never, Obatala! Sango will do no such thing! So, if I were you, I would be begging Death to do the needful. But your case is like that ugly man at Ogbomosho who refused to die despite aging four hundred years, rather he bargained with Death that he would kill all his twenty children—one by one—for him to stay alive till eternity. But that is not possible! How did the man die, Sango?

SANGO: *(acting surprised)*. Oh, you mean that old fool?

ESHU: Oh, yes!

SANGO: What did you expect? I cut off his coconut head, and to date, Oya uses his skull to bathe. One of the things women can do, you know?

OGUN: Can you imagine!

*[Entering, Oya.]*

OYA: *(appeasing Sango)*. Sango, my husband, I pray, please temper justice with mercy. Please release Obatala to go home to his people. Please, my lord, I beg of you. Remember that a man who does not allow anger to lord over him is usually bestowed upon healthy semen by a benevolent spirit to make plenty of babies. *(Kneeling in humility.)*

SANGO: *(rebuffs sharply)*. No, woman! *(Now, raging.)* Do not dare to plead for him, Oya! I forbid you. Go back to your room! Go, woman!

*[Oya hurriedly leaves.]*

SANGO: *(striping himself bare amidst anger)*. Obatala, I, Sango, have vowed to hold you in perpetual bondage as long as I lord over Ile-Ife. I, Sango, single-handedly deposed over four hundred gods and mounted on this throne without fear or favor. And anybody who dares to question that shall be consumed in Sango's wildfire. Sango o! Hmm! *(Panting furiously.)*

*[Meanwhile, Ogun and Eshu frown pensively at Sango's self-adulating.]*

*[Entering, Royal Bard.]*

ROYAL BARD: *(thundering Sango's name)*. Sango, Oko Oya o! Sango, husband of Oya o! *(Thunders again more intensely.)* Sango o! Evil does not lord over a wise man! *(Thunders the third time, now, calmy.)* Kabieyesi o! I pray, may your reign bring positive change to the people of Ife!

SANGO: *(turns to the Royal Bard in anger)*. Enough, madman! And if you dare me one more time by not sheathing your wagging tongue, then you will leave me with no other option than to cut off your head and feed it to the dogs. Fool!

*[Sango smashes the calabash on the floor and then drops on his knees. Now, panting profusely. Meanwhile, Eshu and Ogun maintain their composure.]*

SANGO: *(to Eshu and Ogun)*. Brothers, please, cool me; anger runs in my ancestral bloodline. And please, do not let it get to my head and burst it open! Oluweri—water spirit—cool me! Softly… softly, the snow cools the earth!

*[Ogun and Eshu furrow their brows before going to bathe Sango with water. They return to their seats and then resume sipping their wine.]*

*[Presently, the scene cuts to fresh action entirely at down-stage right as Sango, Eshu, and Ogun transfix. Sanya and Banjo enter, melding their fishnets.]*

BANJO: *(singing)*. Laiye Olugbon… Laiye Aresa… *(Sanya joins in, but Banjo soon restrains.)* Sanya, keep quiet! Stop, I say!

SANYA: W-what? *(Stops melding to pay attention.)* What is it, Banjo?

BANJO: Please, can you stop singing?

SANYA: But you started it.

BANJO: I know, but please...

SANYA: All right. But I hope all is well?

BANJO: *(fires up)*. Why should it be well, when one cannot even boast of one square meal a day, eh, Sanya?

SANYA: I know! Moreover, there is something I am also aware of lately, Banjo. I mean, have you not noticed what has been happening around here lately?

BANJO: And which is? I mean, not that I know of, Sanya. Well, humor me?

SANYA: Are you kidding me? You mean, you have not wondered why the rivers are now stingy like an old man's tears lately?

BANJO: Of course, this year is the worst of it all—no doubt!

SANYA: Can you imagine! I can tell you that since the fishing season started, it has been bad, and in fact, we have not experienced plenty of kills as we had experienced last year and the year after that and the one after that.

BANJO: And you think I would be surprised? Well, I expected even more badly than what we are experiencing right now. Of course, Yemaja—the goddess of the seas and the rivers—would be angry for the imprisonment of her husband. In a saner clime, that is what every good wife would do. Look, you can play with a woman's breasts or buttocks, but never dare what is dearest to her heart. Besides, Obatala is a man every woman would die for to grace her bed. But now, he is in trouble!

SANYA: It is Sango, right?

BANJO: Who else if not the fire-breathing god? I tell you. Sango is the originator of our problems in Ile-Ife.

*[Sango, Eshu, and Ogun furrow their brows.]*

SANYA: What a fraud! Sango, a mare stranger, now lord over us. It is madness, and the world seems to end soon.

*[Eshu and Ogun savor the lampoon heaps on Sango.]*

BANJO: Can you ever imagine that! The world is sick indeed! I can tell you that, my friend. And what angers me most of the time is the involvement of the two rascals who connived with Sango to imprison Obatala to date.

SANYA: It is a pity! Why not!

BANJO: In fact, it was Sango's idea that the world should be altered by a proxy: weapons were made by Ogun in the time passed to kill animals for the pleasure of it. But today, animals like Sango, Eshu, and Ogun use these weapons to kill men for an unjust cause for the business of war.

SANYA: And the funniest thing is that Eshu and Ogun are just mere stooges for Sango. He uses them like laborers without wages to carry out his nefarious action against innocent people like you and me.

BANJO: You mean, Sango does not give a hoot about his friends?

SANYA: I am telling you that Sango does not care about anybody, let alone fools like Eshu and Ogun.

BANJO: Are they that so foolish?

SANYA: In fact, being foolish is an understatement.

*[Sango laughs at Eshu and Ogun derisively.]*

BANJO: And do you blame them? I guess not. I rather blame Sanpanna—god of smallpox—and Obaluaiye—god of the earth—who deserted Obatala in time of need. Obatala who stood for the people so that Orunmila would bless them with wisdom became a victim too soon. Now, they clamor for change because the government of Sango is a sheer dictatorship. Pity, why not.

SANYA: The gods must be crazy indeed! What baffles me is that Sango has vowed to destroy everything Obatala had labored for! And as things stand right now, one does not know whom to trust anymore. (*Throws down the net.*)

[*Action returns to Sango who is by now swollen with anger.*]

SANGO: (*rises in anger*). My father once said, "When an enemy invades, you do not hesitate to show him the steel." (*Turns sharply to Ogun.*) Ogun?

OGUN: I am here, Sango.

SANGO: Where are the weapons you brought for sales?

OGUN: They are here… (*drops the swords before Sango*); there you go.

SANGO: Good! (*Now, turns to Eshu.*) Eshu, you and I know that "patience" has a slender body. So, I have been patient enough listening to the madness of those two. Now, you have to cause confusion between them… Ogun will give you the best weapons for this course other than your termite-eaten club. (*Smiles.*)

ESHU: (*dissatisfies somewhat*): Well, consider it done, Sango! (*Feigning a burst of laughter.*)

[*Eshu springs up suddenly; he quickly wears a long garment: the front of the garment is red, while the back is pitch black. Now, he picks up two swords and stealthily goes to drop them close to where the fishermen are mending their nets and then begins to move to and fro so that they, the fishermen, can see him somewhat like a speed of light.*]

BANJO: *(abruptly drops the net as he looks at Eshu as he goes away)*. Sanya, did you see the man in black that just passed here?

SANYA: *(drops the net)*. You must be kidding me, Banjo! Well, the man that just passed here was in a red.

BANJO: That was a lie!

SANYA: I swear, I saw him with my two naked eyes; he was wearing a red garment from the head down his ankle. Do not be a fool, Banjo.

BANJO: *(eyes red)*. Even so, must you call me a fool?

SANYA: Oh, yes! You are such a crazy fool, because that fellow I saw was wearing a red garment, and you are here arguing with me.

BANJO: You are an irredeemable liar, Sanya. I can bet my life on the fact that that fellow was wearing a black garment from the head down to his ankle. Well, I am not going to continue to argue with a slave like you.

SANYA: *(fires up)*. Did you just call me a slave?

BANJO: Yes, I did. I can even insult your miserable parents if need be. In fact, they are slaves! So now, what are you going to do to me, huh?

SANYA: You are asking me what I am going to do to you?

BANJO: Yes, you heard me. So, what are you going to do… fight me?

SANYA: Listen, Banjo, you can insult me as long as you can relish that, but dragging my parents to the sludge of an insult, that I will die first. *(Now, picking up a sword and starts brandishing it.)* Banjo! Say your last prayer before I cut off your head and feed it to the fishes!

BANJO: You lie, Sanya! *(Picking a sword, too)*. Strike me if you think you have balls beneath your thighs!

*[Sanya and Banjo attack each other fiercely till both of them embrace death.]*

*[Sango, Eshu, and Ogun begin to laugh sinisterly.]*

SANGO: *(still laughing)*. A child, who beats the Igbim drum, does that in preparation for his death. *(Continues laughing.)* Thank you, Eshu.

ESHU: It is a pleasure to carry out your bid, Sango. *(Somewhat angry.)*

SANGO: Ogun, there you go… go and take a bath in the pool of blood. Have fun!

*[They resume their sinister laughter.]*

ROYAL BARD: *(from afar he thunders again)*. Sango o! Hmm! *(Stops abruptly as Sango frowns at him.)*

*SANGO: (to Royal Bard).* I will still be one to cut off your head—mark my words! Fool!

*[Presently, Ogun's business associate enters amidst a laud cry. Ogun approaches him to enquire what the problem is.]*

OGUN: *(enquiring)*. What happened? What happened?

MAN: *(squeaks)*. T-the market is on fire… *(mumbling)* um… and…

OGUN: *(cut in anxiously)*. And what?

MAN: And everything is gone! *(Tearing up profusely.)*

OGUN: *(Starts to sob.)* Argh! Argh!

SANGO: Take heart, my friend. But do not forget you are a god! *(Exchanges glances with Eshu.)*

*[Ogun's eyes are red; he becomes furious in anger. Now, he turns sharply towards Eshu, walking towards him.]*

ESHU: I did not do it! I swear! You have to calm down, Ogun!

OGUN: Do not tell me that, Eshu! I warned you to distance yourself from any form of acrobatic xenophobia… *(tossing Eshu a sword)*, and any smirk of heartlessness and gymnastic hypercriticism. But you did not listen. Charge!

*[Ogun and Eshu begin to fight fiercely. They continue until both of them exit the stage. Meanwhile, Sango has been laughing at the scenario all the while.]*

*CURTAIN*

# The Vendetta of the Gods
## Movement Ten

*Before Sango's palace: market women in semi-nudity attire, marching to Sango's palace, chanting revolutionary songs, and unanimously demanding for the impeachment of Sango.*

ROYAL BARD: *(running and falling while calling Sango)*. Kabieyesi? Kabieyesi?

SANGO: *(storms out with an ax amidst panting)*. I am up here, coward! Now, tell me, what is this rumor I hear?

ROYAL BARD: *(mumbling in fear)*. Ka-bie-ye-si. *(Now, speechless)*. Argh! Argh!

SANGO: Are you normal? Cannot you speak!? Or are you being gagged with smelly female underwear!? What is "argh, argh"!? Speak at once!

ROYAL BARD: Argh, Kabieyesi!

SANGO: *(raging as he points his ax at him)*. By the power of Sango, I command you to speak!

ROYAL BARD: *(mumbling)*. K-Kabieyesi, it is not about commanding me to speak that is so important right now!

SANGO: *(still pointing his ax at him)*. Then do you want to die?

ROYAL BARD: *(now, fidgeting)*. N-not at all, Kabieyesi.

SANGO: *(still pointing his ax at him)*. Then what did you mean? Speak!

ROYAL BARD: Kabieyesi, you are on fire!

SANGO: *(retrieves to pride himself)*. Of course, I am always on fire. But forgive me for not leaping for joy. Huge manhood, you know?

ROYAL BARD: *(yells)*. I mean, your palace is on fire, Kabieyesi!

*[The market women's chant now build to a crescendo. Sango becomes impatient.]*

SANGO: *(self-adulation)*. I am Sango, son of Oranmiyan! Nobody dares to spit out a fire like the god of thunder and lightning! When Sango kills, nobody dares to confront him! *(Turns sharply to the Royal Bard.)* So, who are the dogs ranting before my palace?

ROYAL BARD: *(mumbling)*. T-the market women, Kabieyesi.

SANGO: Really!?

ROYAL BARD: That was what I was trying to tell you, Kabieyesi.

SANGO: I thought as much. Well, go out there and tell them that I, Sango, said they should leave my palace and go home! Otherwise, I will not be nice when I get pushed to the wall. *(Now, tosses his staff to the Royal Bard to take along with him.)*

ROYAL BARD: Argh, Kabieyesi! *(Returning Sango's staff to him.)*

SANGO: What is it!? Are you normal at all!? Oh! I can see you trying to send me an errand instead? Or are you trying to refuse my command, and then think you would be alive to tell the story to your children how you had one time refused to carry out Sango's simple task?

ROYAL BARD: None of the above, Kabieyesi.

SANGO: You think you can disrespect a god like me! Do you? Or have you forgotten who you are?

ROYAL BARD: That is not it, Kabieyesi.

SANGO: *(mimicking)*. That is not it, Kabieyesi. If that is not, what is it then?

ROYAL BARD: *(becoming agitated)*. I-I am sorry! I-I do not think I can… *(pauses, hesitating somewhat)* all right. It is okay. But Kabieyesi, on second thought, have you considered what these women are agitated for? I mean, if you ask me—

SANGO: *(cuts in angrily)*. I do not care! Who do they think they are?! When I first came to this land—you are my alibi—it was like a deserted island that had been ravaged by war for so many years. The following day I became the king of this town; I sprang to work to rebuild this kingdom from scratch. I made her into the state of the art she is today. Business has been good, too. *(Gestures to show little quantity.)* Just because of the little raise in tax, they are threatening me with fire and brimstone. And as disrespectful as it seems, they are also demanding for my impeachment as if their great-grandfathers participated in some sort of election that brought me on this throne. How daft human beings can be sometimes!

*[A Guard rushes in panting.]*

GUARD: *(kneeling before Sango)*. My, Lord!

SANGO: What is it, Ajanaku?

GUARD: My lord, this is no longer an agitation. These people just killed one of our own. So, what do you want me to do?

SANGO: You are a fool! You are asking me what I want you to do? In fact, you are a bunch of fools! *(Kicking him a couple of times.)* Nonsense!

ROYAL BARD: Take it easy, Kabieyesi.

SANGO: *(cuts in sharply)*. What am I taking it easy, uh?

ROYAL BARD: *(fear grips him)*. Y-your anger, Kabieyesi.

SANGO: You are a bigger fool! If he had remembered the rules of engagement, we would not have been having this conversation right now.

ROYAL BARD: *(mumbling)*. A-and what could that be, Kabieyesi, if you do not mind me—

SANGO: *(cuts sharply)*. He ought to have cut off the heads of those women before coming here to tell me rubbish!

ROYAL BARD: *(reprimanding Sango)*. Argh, Kabieyesi!

SANGO: *(fires at the royal Bard)*. It is that "Argh, Kabieyesi" that will send you to your early grave! Fools!

ROYAL BARD: My apologies, Kabieyesi.

SANGO: Apologies, my ass! *(Fires up again)*. How dare the children of Obatala demand for Sango's wrath in such a trying time? *(To Guard sharply.)* Listen, go straight to the tax collector's house and tell him that I, Sango, said he should double the taxes. No. Tell him I said I want it to be tripled! Go!

*[The Guard leaves.]*

SANGO: *(to the Royal Bard)*. Meanwhile, you still need to go out there and warn those dogs to leave my palace this minute. I have been patient enough. Now, go! *(Vibrating angrily)*.

ROYAL BARD: *(mumbling)*. B-but Kabieyesi, I doubt if these women would leave this palace ten years to come.

SANGO: *(demands pungently)*. Why, if I may ask!?

ROYAL BARD: Because they are saying that their strengths lie in their determinations to be heard and that if they do not get what they are clamoring for, they would rather die here than go home unfulfilled. Can you imagine!

SANGO: Then I will make sure their dying wish comes to pass!

*[Presently, market women entering amidst indistinct chanting. Now, Sango more impatient.]*

SANGO: *(addressing Royal Bard)*. What is the meaning of this? What is the meaning of this madness?

ROYAL BARD: I do not understand, too, Kabieyesi.

IYALOJA: *(clenching her fists to quiet the noise)*. Thank you, my fellow women. *(She turns to Sango)*. Kabieyesi o! *(Readjusting her wrapper)*. Kabieyesi, our people say, "A man who brings home an ant-infested faggot should not complain if he is visited by a lounge of lizards." So—

SANGO: *(cuts in angrily)*. Speak no further, Iyaloko, or whatever they named you!

ROYAL BARD: *(cuts in whispering)*. It is "Iyaloja," Kabieyesi.

SANGO: *(firing again)*. Whatever it is, I do not care! What I am saying is that I do not want to hear a word from that filthy thing she calls a mouth!

IYALOJA: Kabieyesi, listen to me, I want to talk to you!

SANGO: *(addressing Royal Bard).* Just imagine the audacity!

ROYAL BARD: It is nothing, Kabieyesi.

SANGO: *(rages).* You are a fool if you think that was nothing!

ROYAL BARD: My apologies, Kabieyesi!

SANGO: Apologies, my ass! *(Turns sharply to the market women.)* Listen to me…

IYALOJA: *(cuts in angrily).* No! You listen to me, Kabieyesi! For crying out loud, what is wrong with your head?

*[Murmuring from the market women rents the air.]*

SANGO: Silence! Silence, I say! *(Now, addressing Iyaloja.)* I do not know what you are trying to do, but whatever it is, it is not going to work here! Do you hear me? Moreover, I loathe the sight of every floppy breast I am seeing before my own very eyes. Oya's breasts have weighed better. Now, go home!

IYALOJA: We will not, Kabieyesi! We are saying "Enough is enough," Kabieyesi!

MARKET WOMEN: *(chorus).* Enough is enough, Kabieyesi!

IYALOJA: Kabieyesi, we are saying: "Enough of the huge taxes you are forcing on our throats." We are also saying: "Release Obatala to us but if you cannot consider or reconsider our proposal, then you should step down, Kabieyesi!" *(Addressing the market women).* Have I spoken your minds?

MARKET WOMEN: *(they chorus).* Oh, yes!

IYALOJA: That was all, Sango! *(Genuflecting.)*

SANGO: *(firing up as he turns to the Royal Bard).* Oh, did you hear her? She just called me by my first name! Blasphemy! Blasphemy! *(Calling.)* Oya? Oya?

*[She storms out.]*

OYA: You called, Kabieyesi?

SANGO: Oya, give me my thunderbolt charm!

OYA: *(agitating).* B-but Kabieyesi, please, I think you have to calm down.

SANGO: *(sharply, firing up)* Do not tell me to calm down, Oya! Do not tell me that! Just give me what I asked of you—now!

OYA: Okay, okay, I heard you!

*[Oya is inserting her fingers inside her womanliness to bring out Sango's charm.]*

SANGO: Hurry up, Oya! And also, I want you to drop down the weeping sky! This is war! This is war!

ILALOJA: Come on, Sango, you are such a crying baby! Do you see any of us warring with you here? Our demands had been stated clearly, so we are waiting for you to make a wise decision as a wise man would do in this kind of situation. But if you prove to be otherwise, then you will leave us with no other option than to force you to abdicate the throne of our forefathers.

SANGO: *(fires up).* Insolence!

OYA: *(finally fetches the charm out).* Take, Kabieyesi.

SANGO: *(collects it).* Why is it so wet?

OYA: I do not know, Kabieyesi! B-but I am sure it still has its potency intact.

SANGO: Are you sure?

OYA: I am sure it has, Kabieyesi.

SANGO: It better be! *(Now, he swallows it.)* Now, conjure the rain!

OYA: I cannot, Kabieyesi!

SANGO: *(he is dumbfounded).* W-why? What happened? *(Thunders.)* Oya!?

OYA: I do not know, Kabieyesi. *(Kneeling before Sango.)* I have been trying to conjure rain a couple of nights ago in order to usher in the planting season, but all my efforts had been in vain.

SANGO: *(becoming more frustrated).* Oh, no! Oya, not when there is a war in the palace. You have to try again and again.

*[Oya carries a water pot, tries to conjure rain, but nothing is working out.]*

OYA: I still cannot, Kabieyesi. It seems Omo Luweri—the water goddess—is refusing to grant my request for conjuring the cloudless sky. Just take a look… *(Drops the water pot at the feet of Sango.)* Do you see what I am talking about?

SANGO: *(staring into the water pot more closely).* Yemaja o! *(Whirling.)* Yemaja? I can sight your conspiracy! But do not worry, we will see who will laugh the longest! *(Turns to the market women sharply.)* Now, listen, you snobby fallen women: I am giving you my last warning; go home and start thinking how you can get your levies paid. *(Thunders).* Now, you may leave my palace!

MARKET-WOMEN: *(chorus).* Not until you step down, Sango! We will rather die here than go home! Enough is enough, Sango!

*[Indistinct chattering. Now, Sango is in rage as he breaks the waterpot.]*

SANGO: *(begins to brandish his ax amidst incantations).* A child that plays with the testicles of his father while sleeping shall be blinded by akalamagbo— hornbill. The snake that rivals the Dane gun shall be killed by the Dane gun! *(Now, losing his temper, pronouncing his name in rage.)* Sango o! Hmm! *(Panting furiously.)*

IYALOJA: That is, it? You are a coward, Sango!

*[Now, Sango is in rage as his countenance changes. Royal Bard leaves Sango to join the women.]*

SANGO: *(he exclaims in surprise as he sees Eoyal Bard).* You, too?

ROYAL BARD: What do you think, Kabieyesi? Well, our people say, "Praying against the falling of an overripe fruit is not spirituality; it is stupidity."

SANGO: Meaning…?

ROYAL BARD: *(explaining placidly).* Meaning, Kabieyesi, if a few people speak against you, it is normal; but if everybody speaks evil about you, then you are evil. So, no amount of freezing can reverse the rottenness of a rotten fish. I am sorry, Kabieyesi!

SANGO: *(fires up).* Sorry for yourself! Fool! Anyway, I have heard enough of your insubordinations. So, whatever happens from this moment on will be your doom—all of you!

IYALOJA: So, are you going to kill us all? *(Readjusting her wrapper.)* Are you not ashamed of yourself?

SANGO: *(pointing his ax upward to ignite thunderclap).* Sango o!

*[It is assumed that a thunderbolt kills a few of the market women, while others take to their heels. Presently, Obatala wakes up from his slumber to what Sango has done.]*

OBATALA: *(thunders)*. Argh! Sango! Horror! How could you, Sango? *(Lamenting, then looks upward)*. Eledua, can you see that Sango has finally lost his godhead! *(Now, feigning a peal of ridiculous laughter.)*

SANGO: *(yelling at Obatala)*. Stop laughing, Obatala! *(Squeezing Obatala's jaw tightly, then yells again.)* Have you seen what you have caused? Huh? And you think that was funny!? Fool! That is what you are! *(Disengaging.)*

OBATALA: *(gasping for air)*. You think you can mock me, Sango, like the proverbial monkey that laughs when a big tree falls, not knowing that it is his house that is falling? But you have failed both here and hereafter, Sango. Posterity will judge you! *(Now, screaming loud)*. Horror! Horror!

*[Sango turns sharply towards the entrance as Ilesanmi enters.]*

SANGO: *(to Ilesanmi)*. Have I not warned you not to come back here? *(Thunders.)* Do you want to die!?

ILESANMI: *(looking at the full moon. Now, he blurts out)*. Sango o! Womì d'ada ki'o tu' miwo—Look at me eyeball to eyeball—Sango. Listen, a god had never met his untimely death in my bloodless hands before, but I would not budge this time sending you over: either to the world beyond or to the forest of thousand demons where your kinds wander the earth aimlessly. Sango, in the time of Olugbon and Aresa, an elderly woman would not be at home while the she-goat suffered parturition.

SANGO: Meaning…

ILESANMI: Meaning you are a coward! Hubris! I am telling you to step down, Sango!

SANGO: Never!

ILESANMI: Sango, do you know that a woman does not womanize, neither does a man menstruate?

SANGO: That I know, so what is your point?

ILESANMI: The point is that your time is up!

SANGO: *(laughing cynically)*. You are such a poophead, you know? Well, I suggest you go home this minute, young man!

ILESANMI: Never! Sango, the gentility of a tiger should not be taken for cowardice. *(Cuts his palm with a knife.)* Sango, I swear by the blood that is streaming down you have met your doom today! *(Thunders)*. Sango o!

SANGO: That was it? *(Laughing deliriously)*. You are a madman! It is apparent madness runs in your lineage. *(To Oya, who stands watching.)* Fetch me a strong rope, woman; this madman needs to be tied up before he goes about causing more trouble!

ILESANMI: No need for that, Sango, because I came prepared to bring you down on your knees!

SANGO: Is that so?

ILESANMI: It is so, Sango!

SANGO: Then prepare to die!

ILESANMI: You lie, Sango! Listen, eni t oba f oju ana w oku, ebora a bo laso—Whoever commonizes a ghost for the living shall be haunted by a malevolent spirit! *(Fetching out a sword in preparation for a fight.)*

SANGO: I see! Listen arakunrin—brother—one does not test the depths of a river with both feet. But you just did. What a pity! (*Now, he turns to Oya sharply.*) Fetch me my sword!

OYA: (*fetches it and then gives it to Sango*). Here it is, Kabieyesi.

ILESANMI: Come down and fight, Sango, if you think you have testicles beneath your thighs! (*Brandishing his sword.*)

SANGO: (*raging*). Imagine the audacity! You are next!

ILESANMI: Then fight me! (*Vibrating vigorously.*)

[*Sango removes the sword from the sheath, then advances towards Ilesanmi fiercely.*]

SANGO: Charge!

ILESANMI: Charge!

[*They start fighting till both swords break amidst panting*]

[*Sango slits a cockerel, drinks its blood, and then sprinkles some blood on metals.*]

SANGO: (*conjuring*). Ogun, when a mother hears the cries of her child, she races to attend to the child. (*Thunders.*) Ogun o! I need you to forge me an indestructible sword. Appear! (*Opening a smoked pot which assaults the arena, but Ogun does not appear.*)

OBATALA: (*laughing*). Call him again, Sango! Perhaps, the fool might be sleeping after so much bathing he must have had in that pool of blood in his backyard. (*Racking his brain in suggestion.*) Okay. Why not call Eshu Odara, who does not think twice before he strikes an innocent being? Well, if you ask me, I will suggest you take the honorable bow and step down from the throne! But would your ego allow you, eh, Sango? (*Resumes laughing deliriously.*)

SANGO: *(to Obatala)*. Thanks, but no thanks! *(To Ilesanmi.)* Arakunrin o? Ilesanmi o?

ILESANMI: *(self-adulation)*. It is a demi-god you are calling, Sango.

SANGO: Better! Then look up and bellow, this is your last day on earth! Because a child that dares an iroko tree shall regret the consequences. A witch that perches on a high tension wire shall not live to partake in a cauldron. Nobody dares the fire in the eyes of Sango and lives to tell the story! *(Striping himself bare, then thunders.)* Sango o! *(Now, he stabs Ilesanmi in the stomach.)* I told you that as long as I am around, you will always be a fool! This is your fate, embrace it! *(Stabbing Ilesanmi the second time.)*

*[Ilesanmi groans in pain as he falls.]*

OBATALA: *(screaming in horror)*. Argh, Sango! Horror!

*[Langbodo enters with two able-bodied men who carry Oyeyemi on a stretcher. Oyeyemi begins to groan as soon as they set her down at the center of the stage. The men leave.]*

LANGBODO: *(goes to attend to Ilesanmi)*. Ilesanmi! *(Turns to Sango sharply.)* Argh, Sango, what have you done?

SANGO: And what do you think I have done?

ILESANMI: *(grabbing Langbodo and whispering to him)*. B-Baba, I-I cannot hold on any longer… They are here… *(dying)* Take care of him…

LANGBODO: *(cuts in surprisingly)*. "Him?"

ILESANMI: Yes, "him." *(Now, starting to cough, and then dies afterward.)*

LANGBODO: Horror! Awuu! Pity!

*[Townspeople enter, and they begin to sing a choral dirge, gradually building to a crescendo as Sango licks the blood that stains his sword. Now, Sango begins to pant. Presently, Oyeyemi begins to undergo labor. The women attend to her; they are over her to deliver the baby. Oyeyemi screams.]*

FIRST WOMAN: Push, Oyeyemi… push!

SECOND WOMAN: Push… that is it!

*[Oyeyemi groans and gives birth. The baby cries.]*

FIRST WOMAN: It is a boy!

*[Townspeople cheers!]*

LANGBODO: May Eledumare—the Creator—be praised! *(Smiling.)*

SECOND WOMAN: *(squeaks so loud)*. Horror!

*[Everybody startles. Oyeyemi is no more. Joy has been cut short. Now, a sad moment blankets the earth. Townspeople begin to hum a choral dirge. Langbodo is furious.]*

LANGBODO: *(thunders)*. Sango? *(Now, setting down the Opele Oracle.)* Sango, confront me eyeball to eyeball if you can! It is the "Opele Oracle" that led the creation story. It is the "Opele Oracle" that divined and cut your umbilical cord and that of other gods at the abyss. That same "Opele Oracle" has come to plague that same fate today. *(Langbodo sits to cast his Opele Oracle)*. Won'di Ifa… fu'n Sango—Ifa Oracle says when Sango's destiny was divined and forged…

SANGO: *(cuts in furiously)*. No o! *(Turning in a circle like a whirled wind)*. No o!

LANGBODO: *(continuing plaquing Sango's destiny)*. Ifa Oracle says when Sango's destiny was divined and forged by Eledua at the abyss of creation….

SANGO: *(crying out in frustration).* No o! *(Now, thunders.)* Eshu o! Ogun o! Hmm! *[Sango stabs himself and dies standing while Oya runs off stage.]*

TOWNSPEOPLE: *(somewhat empathetic).* Oba waja! Pity, why not!

LANGBODO: This is bad omen indeed! However, this too shall pass!

*[Langbodo unties Obatala and crowns him].*

TOWNSPEOPLE: *(chorusing, cheering).* Long live the king! Long live the king!

*[Dancers entering, dancing, and singing].*

OBATALA: *(waving his staff of office).* Esheun! Thank you for your perseverance this far, my people. I must confess, I am elated to witness this renewable transition today. It is a breath of fresh air, I must say to you all. And this can only mean one good thing for us all; it is a new dawn for a new beginning, my people!

TOWNSPEOPLE: *(cheering).* Long live the king! Long live the king!

*[Obatala smears the child's forehead with a whitish substance, crowns him, and then lifts him].*

OBATALA: *(child presentation).* Behold your new king—Obasanjo.

TOWNSPEOPLE: *(bowing).* Kabieyesi o! *(Then rise to chorus).* Long live the king! Long live the king!

ROYAL BARD: *(from afar thundering).* Obasanjo, son of Ilesanmi o!

OBATALA: *(to Royal Bard).* Hold it, Abobaku. *(Turns to Townspeople).* My people, my task as a messenger of Eledua is now complete. So, I will not remain with you any longer because I have to return to Eledua to give an account of my deeds and travesty while lording over Ile-Ife. *(Gently turns to Langbodo).*

Please, give Ilesanmi and Oyeyemi a befitting burial; they were the greatest individuals who had ever walked this part and paid the ultimate price for all. If need be, let Ile-Ife be named after Ilesanmi—he was a great man! I do not think you understand?

LANGBODO: *(bows)*. I do, my lord. I will make sure everything you said is carried out perfectly.

OBATALA: I am glad to hear that, Langbodo. Well, do not forget to smash three raw eggs on Sango's forehead as tradition demands for anyone who dies standing. You do know the ritual?

LANGBODO: I do, my lord. I will see to it at once! *(Fetching out three eggs and then smashes them on Sango's forehead)*.

OBATALA: *(singling two men out)*. You and... you. No. You, yes... give the old man a hand to drop the dead man. *(They obey)*. Gently... *(dropping Sango down gently)* aha! That is, it! Do not forget he was a king. *(Exiting the stage.)* Do not forget he was a god. *(Now, exits finally.)*

ROYAL BARD: *(eulogizing)*. Sango o! Ajanaku subu ko le dide. Ologbo sun o dabi ole! Erin subu, igbo dakeke. Sango, o dile koko, o da arinako, o ma to di inu ala. Ti o ba de orun, kio se orun re! May Eledua forgive your wrongdoings and grant you safe passage to the afterlife! Adieu!

# Epilogue

[Presently, drum sound builds up from the background to a crescendo, ushering Townpeople into the mood of dancing.]

*THE END*